"What if you get in trouble?" She stared into his face, wishing he'd reconsider and take her along. **"What if you're hurt?"**

He smiled, his hand cupping her cheek. "Worried about me?"

Jacie stiffened and had a retort ready on her lips, but stopped short of delivering it when she realized she was worried about him. "I haven't known you long, but damn it, I am worried about you. I kinda got used to having you around." Her hand covered the one he'd used to cup her cheek and she pulled it lower, pressing a kiss into his palm.

"Stay safe for me, will you?" His eyes dark in the dim lighting from the overhead bulbs, he leaned close and captured her lips in a soul-stealing kiss.

Dear Harlequin Intrigue Reader,

For nearly thirty years fearless romance has fueled every Harlequin Intrigue book. Now we want everyone to know about the great crime stories our fantastic authors write and the variety of compelling miniseries we offer. We think our new cover look complements and enhances our promise to deliver edge-of-your-seat reads in all six of our titles—and brand-new titles every month!

This month's lineup is packed with nonstop mystery in *Smoky Ridge Curse,* the third in Paula Graves's Bitterwood P.D. trilogy, exciting action in *Sharpshooter,* the next installment in Cynthia Eden's Shadow Agents miniseries, and of course fearless romance—whether from newcomers Jana DeLeon and HelenKay Dimon or veteran author Aimée Thurlo, we've got every angle covered.

Next month buckle up as Debra Webb returns with a new Colby Agency series featuring The Specialists. And in November *USA TODAY* bestselling author B.J. Daniels takes us back to "The Canyon" for her special *Christmas at Cardwell Ranch* celebration.

Lots going on and lots more to come. Be sure to check out www.Harlequin.com for what's coming next.

Enjoy,

Denise Zaza

Senior Editor

Harlequin Intrigue

TAKING AIM

—

ELLE JAMES

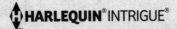

This book is dedicated to the brave men and women
who risk their lives daily fighting
for truth and justice.

Recycling programs
for this product may
not exist in your area.

ISBN-13: 978-0-373-74760-3

TAKING AIM

Copyright © 2013 by Mary Jernigan

Printed in U.S.A.

ABOUT THE AUTHOR

A Golden Heart Award winner for Best Paranormal Romance in 2004, Elle James started writing when her sister issued a Y2K challenge to write a romance novel. She has managed a full-time job and raised three wonderful children, and she and her husband even tried their hands at ranching exotic birds (ostriches, emus and rheas) in the Texas Hill Country. Ask her, and she'll tell you what it's like to go toe-to-toe with an angry 350-pound bird! After leaving her successful career in information technology management, Elle is now pursuing her writing full-time. Elle loves to hear from fans. You can contact her at ellejames@earthlink.net or visit her website at www.ellejames.com.

Books by Elle James

CAST OF CHARACTERS

Zach Adams—Former FBI special agent tortured and broken by Los Lobos cartel.

Jacie Kosart—Big Elk Ranch big game hunting trail guide desperate to find her twin sister.

Tracie Kosart—FBI special agent kidnapped while on vacation visiting her sister on the Big Elk Ranch.

Hank Derringer—Billionaire willing to take the fight for justice into his own hands by setting up CCI—Covert Cowboys, Inc.

Bruce Masterson—Tracie Kosart's fiancé and fellow FBI special agent.

Richard Giddings—Owner of Big Elk Ranch game hunting operation.

Humberto Hernandez—Big Elk Ranch trail guide who knew more than he should have.

Cara Jo Smith—Pretty single woman who owns the diner in Wild Oak Canyon.

Enrique Sanchez—La Familia Diablos gang member.

Juan Alvarez—Tracie's contact who informed her of the coming transfer in Wild Horse Canyon.

Brandon Pendley—Hank Derringer's computer guru.

Grant Lehmann—Hank Derringer's old friend and big dog in the FBI.

Chapter One

Zachary Adams sat with his boots tapping the floor, his attention barely focused on the man at the center of the group of cowboys. This meeting had gone past his fifteen-minute limit, pushing twenty now.

The wiry, muscular man before them stood tall, his shoulders held back and proud. He was probably a little older than most of the men in the room, his dark hair combed back, graying slightly at the temples.

"I'm here to offer you a position in a start-up corporation." Hank Derringer smiled at the men gathered in the spacious living room of his home on the Raging Bull Ranch in south Texas.

"Doing what? Sweeping floors? Who wants a bunch of rejects?" Zach continued tapping his foot, itching for a fight, his hands shaking. Not that there had been any provocation. He didn't need any. Ever since the catastrophe of the Diego Operation, he hadn't been able to sit still for long, unless he was nursing a really strong bottle of tequila.

"*I* need you. Because you aren't rejects, you're just the type of men I'm looking for. Men who will fight for what you believe in, who were born or raised on a ranch, with the ethics and strength of character of a good cowboy. I'm inviting you to become a part of CCI, known only to those on the inside as Covert Cowboys Incorporated, a specialized team of citizen soldiers, bodyguards, agents and ranch hands who will do whatever it takes for justice."

Zach almost laughed out loud. Hank had flipped if he thought this crew of washed-up cowboys could help him start up a league of justice or whatever it was he had in mind.

"Whoa, back up a step there. Covert Cowboys Incorporated?" The man Hank had introduced as Chuck Bolton slapped his hat against his thigh. "Sounds kind of corny to me. What's the punch line?"

"No punch line." Hank squared his shoulders, his mouth firming into a straight line. "Let's just say that I'm tired of justice being swept under the rug."

Ex-cop Ben Harding shook his head. "I'm not into circumventing the law."

"I'm not asking you to. The purpose of Covert Cowboys Incorporated is to provide covert protection and investigation services where hired guns and the law aren't enough." Hank's gaze swept over the men in the room. "I handpicked each of you because you are all highly skilled soldiers, cops and agents who know how to work hard and fire a gun and are familiar with living on the edge of danger. My plan is to inject you into situations where your own lives could be on the line to protect, rescue or ferret out the truth."

One by one, the cowboys agreed to sign on with CCI until Hank came to Zach.

"I'm not much into joining," Zach said.

Hank nodded. "To be understood. You might not want to get back into a job that puts you in the line of fire after what you went through."

Zach's chest tightened. "I'm not afraid of bullets."

"I understand you lost your female partner on your last mission with the FBI. That had to be tough." Hank laid a hand on Zach's shoulder. "You're welcome to stay the night and think about it. You don't have to give me an answer until morning."

Zach could have given his answer now. He didn't want the job. He didn't want any job. What he wanted was revenge, served cold and painful.

With the other cowboys falling in line, Zach just nodded, grabbed his duffel bag and found the room he had been assigned for the night. The other men left, one of them already on assignment, and the other two had places to stay in Wild Oak Canyon, the small town closest to the Raging Bull Ranch.

Zach hadn't been in the bedroom more than three minutes when the walls started closing in around him. He had to get outside or go crazy.

The room had French doors opening out onto the wide veranda that wrapped around the entire house.

He sat on the steps leading down off the porch at the side of the rambling homestead and stared up at a sky full of the kind of stars you only got out in the wide-open spaces far away from city lights.

Zach wondered if the stars had been out that night Toni had died. No matter how often he replayed that nightmare, he couldn't recall whether or not the stars had been shining. Everything seemed to play out in black, white and red. From the moment they'd been surrounded by the cartel sentinels to the moment Toni had died.

Zach's eyes squeezed shut, but no matter how hard he tried to erase the vision from his mind, he couldn't shake it. He opened his eyes again and looked up at the stars in an attempt to superimpose their beauty and brilliance over the ugly images indelibly etched in his memory.

Boots tapped against the planks of the decking

and Hank Derringer leaned against a wooden column. "Wanna talk about it?"

"No." Zach had suffered through days of talking about it with the FBI psychologist following his escape and return to civilization. Talking hadn't brought his partner back, and it had done nothing to bring justice to those responsible for her senseless rape, torture and murder.

"Do you have work lined up when you leave here?" Hank asked.

"No." Oh, he had work, all right. He had spent the last year following his recovery searching for the cartel gang who'd captured him and Toni Gutierrez on the wrong side of the border during the cartel eradication push, Operation Diego.

The operation had been a failure from the get-go, leading Zach to believe they had a mole inside the FBI. No matter who he asked or where he dug, he couldn't get to the answer. His obsession with the truth had ultimately cost him his job. When his supervisor had given him an ultimatum to pull his head out of his search and get on with his duties as a special agent or look for alternative employment, Zach had walked.

Out of leads, his bank account dwindling and at the mercy of this crackpot vigilante, Hank Derringer, Zach was running out of options.

Zach sighed and stared down the shadowy road leading through a stand of scrub trees toward the highway a mile away. What choice did he have? Crawl into a bottle and forget everything? Even that required money.

"If I take this job—not saying that I've agreed—what did you have in mind for my first assignment?"

JACIE KOSART AND her twin, Tracie, rode toward the ridgeline overlooking Wild Horse Canyon. The landmark delineated the southern edge of the three-hundred-and-fifty-thousand-acre Big Elk Ranch, where Jacie worked as a trail guide for big-game hunting expeditions.

Tracie, on leave from her job with the FBI, had insisted on coming along as one of the guides, even though she wasn't officially working for Big Elk Ranch. "Don't let on that I'm an agent. I just want to blend in and be like you, one of the guides, for today."

Jacie had cleared it with Richard Giddings, her boss. Then Tracie had insisted on taking on these two guys with short haircuts and poker faces instead of the rednecks from Houston.

Happy to have her sister with her for the day, Jacie didn't argue, just went with the flow. Her job was to lead the hunting party to the best hunting location where they stood a chance of bagging trophy elk.

Instead of following behind, the two men rode

ahead with Jacie and Tracie trailing a couple of horse lengths to their rear.

"I was surprised to see you," Jacie stated. Her sister rarely visited, and her sudden appearance had Jacie wondering if something was wrong.

"I needed some downtime from stress," Tracie responded, her words clipped. She flicked the strands of her long, straight brown hair that had come loose from her ponytail back behind her ears.

Not to be deterred by Tracie's cryptic reply, Jacie dug deeper. "What did Bruce have to say about you coming out here without him?" Jacie had to admit to a little envy that Tracie had a boyfriend and she did not. Living on the Big Elk, surrounded by men, she'd have thought she'd have a bit of a love life. But she didn't.

"I told him I needed time with my only sibling." Tracie gave her a tight smile that didn't quite reach her eyes.

Jacie gave an unladylike snort. "As thick as you two have become, I'm surprised he didn't come with you."

Tracie glanced ahead to the two men. "I wanted to come alone."

Tracie might be telling the truth about wanting to come alone, but her answer wasn't satisfying Jacie. Her twin connection refused to believe it was just a case of missing family. "Everything okay?"

"Sure." She glanced at Jacie. "So, how many guides are there on the Big Elk Ranch?"

The change in direction of the conversation wasn't lost on Jacie, but she let it slide. "There are six, plus Richard. Some of them are part-time. Richard, Humberto and I are the full-timers. Why?"

"Just wondered. What kind of process does Richard use to screen his guides?"

Jacie shot a look at her sister. "What do you mean?"

Tracie looked away. "I was just curious if you and the other guides had to go through a background check."

"I don't know about any background check. Richard offered me the job during my one and only interview. I can't vouch for the rest." Jacie frowned at Tracie. "Thinking about giving up the FBI to come guide on the Big Elk?" She laughed, the sound trailing off.

Her sister shrugged. "Maybe."

"No way. You love the FBI. You've wanted to join since you were eight."

"Sometimes you get tired of all the games." Tracie's lips tightened. "We should catch up with them." She nudged her horse, ending the conversation and leaving Jacie even more convinced her sister wasn't telling her everything.

Tracie rode up alongside the men.

Jacie caught up and put on her trail-guide smile as they pulled to a halt at the rim of the canyon. "This is the southern edge of the ranch. The other hunting party is to the west, the Big Elk Ranch house and barn is to the north where we came from, and to the east is the Raging Bull Ranch." Jacie smiled at the two men who'd paid a hefty sum to go hunting that day on the ranch. Richard, her boss, had taken the guys from Houston west; these two had insisted on going south, stating they preferred a lot of distance between them and the other hunting parties.

Jacie and Tracie knew the trophy bucks preferred the western and northern edge of the spread, but the two men would not be deterred.

Supposedly they'd come to hunt, based on the hardware they'd packed in their scabbards. Each carried a rifle equipped with a high-powered scope and a handgun in case they were surprised by javelinas, the vicious wild hogs running wild in the bush.

Jacie cleared her throat, breaking the silence. "Now that you've seen quite a bit of the layout, where would you like to set up? It's getting late and we won't have much time to hunt before sunset."

Jim Smith glanced across at his buddy Mike Jones.

Mr. Jones slipped a GPS device from his pocket

and studied the map on it for a long moment. Then he glanced at Jacie. "Where does that canyon lead?"

"Off the Big Elk Ranch into the Big Bend National Park. There's no hunting allowed in the park. The rangers are pretty strict about it. Not to mention, the border patrol has reported recent drug trafficking activity in this canyon. It's not safe to go in there." And Jacie discouraged their clientele from crossing over the boundaries with firearms, even if their clients were licensed to carry firearms as these two were. All the hunters had been briefed on the rules should they stray into the park.

Jacie's gelding, D'Artagnan, shifted to the left, pawing at the dirt, ready to move on.

"We'll ride farther into the canyon." Mr. Jones nudged his horse's flanks, sending him over the edge of the ridge and down the steep slope toward the canyon.

"Mr. Jones," Tracie called after him. "The horses are property of the Big Elk Ranch. We aren't allowed to take them off the ranch without permission from the boss. Given the dangers that could be encountered, I can't allow you—"

Mr. Smith's horse brushed past Jacie's, following Mr. Jones down the slope. Not a word from either gentleman.

Jacie glanced across at her twin. "What the

heck?" She pulled the two-way radio from her belt and hit the talk switch. "Richard, do you copy?"

The crackle of static had D'Artagnan dancing in place, his head tossing in the air. He liked being in the lead. The two horses descending the slope in front of him made him anxious. He whinnied, calling out to the other horses as the distance between them increased.

The answering whinny from one of the mares below sent the gelding over the edge.

Tracie's mare pranced along the ridge above, her nostrils flared, also disturbed by the departure of the other two horses.

"I'll follow and keep an eye on the two," Tracie suggested.

"Richard, do you copy?" Jacie called into the radio. Apparently they'd moved out of range of radio reception with the other hunting party. Jacie switched frequencies for the base station at the ranch. "Base, this is Jacie, can you read me?"

Again static.

They were on their own and responsible for the two horses and clients headed down into the canyon.

"You feeling weird about this?" Tracie asked.

"You bet."

"Why don't you head back and let Giddings know the clients have left the property? I'll follow along and make sure they don't get lost."

"Not a good idea. You aren't as familiar with the land as I am." Jacie glanced down the trail at the two men on Big Elk Ranch horses. "If they want to get themselves lost or shot, I don't care, but those are Big Elk Ranch horses."

Tracie nodded. "Ginger and Rocky. And you know they like being part of a group, not off on their own." She shook her head. "What are those guys thinking?"

"I don't know, but I don't want to abandon the horses." Jacie sighed. "I guess there's nothing to it but for us to follow and see if we can talk some sense into those dirtbags."

"I'm not liking it," Tracie said. "You should head back and notify Giddings."

"I don't feel right abandoning the horses and I sure as hell won't let you go after them by yourself. We don't know what kind of kooks these guys are." Jacie nodded toward the saddlebags they carried on their horses, filled with first aid supplies, emergency rations and a can of mace. "Look, we're prepared for anything on two or four legs. As long as we keep our heads, we should be okay."

Each woman carried a rifle in her scabbard, for hunting or warding off dangerous animals. They also carried enough ammo for a decent round of target practice in case they didn't actually see any game on the trail, which they hadn't up to this point. Tracie had the added protection of a nine-millimeter Glock she'd carried with her since she left training at Quantico.

"Whatever you say." Tracie grimaced at her. "My rifle's loaded and on safe." She patted the Glock in the holster she'd worn on her hip. "Ready?"

"I don't like it, but let's follow. Maybe we can talk them into returning with us." Jacie squeezed her horse's sides. That's all it took for D'Artagnan to leap forward and start down the winding trail to the base of the canyon.

"Hey, guys! To make it back to camp for supper, we need to head back in the next hour," Jacie called out to the men ahead.

Either they didn't hear her or they chose to ignore her words. The men didn't even look back, just kept going.

D'Artagnan set his own pace on the slippery slope. Jacie didn't urge him to go faster. He wanted to catch up, but he knew his own limits on the descent.

The two men riding ahead worked their way downward at a pace a little faster than Jacie's and Tracie's mounts. At the rate they were moving, they'd have a substantial lead.

Jacie wasn't worried so much about catching up. She knew D'Artagnan and Tracie's gelding, Aramis, were faster than the mare and gelding ahead. But there were many twists and turns in the canyon below. If they didn't catch them soon, they stood a chance of falling even farther behind. It would take them longer to track the two men, and dusk would settle in. Not to mention, it would get dark sooner at the base of the canyon where sunlight disappeared thirty minutes earlier than up top.

As Jacie neared the bottom of the canyon, the two men disappeared past a large outcropping of rock.

D'Artagnan stepped up the pace, stretching into a gallop, eager to catch the two horses ahead. The pounding of hooves reverberated off the walls of the canyons. Tracie and Aramis kept pace behind her. If the two clients had continued at a sedate rate, they would have caught them by now.

The deeper the women traveled into the canyon, the angrier Jacie became at the men. They'd disregarded her warning about drug traffickers and about entering the national park with firearms, and they'd disrespected the fact that the horses didn't belong to them. They were Big Elk Ranch property and belonged on the ranch.

At the first junction, the ground was rocky and disturbed in both directions as if the men had started up one route, turned back and taken the other. In order to determine which route they ended up on, Jacie, the better tracker of the twins, had to dismount and follow their tracks up the dead end and back before she realized it was the other corridor they'd taken.

Tracie stood guard at the fork in case the men returned.

Jacie climbed into the saddle muttering, "We really need to perform a more thorough background check on our clients before we let them onto the ranch."

Her sister smiled. "Not all of them are as disagreeable as these two."

"Yeah, but not only are they putting themselves and the horses in danger, they're putting the two of us at risk, as well." Jacie hesitated. "Come to think of it, maybe we should head back while there's still enough light to climb the trail out of the canyon."

Tracie sighed. "I was hoping you'd say that. I don't want you to get hurt out here."

"Me? I was more concerned about you. You haven't been in the saddle much since you joined the FBI."

"You're right, of course." She smiled at Jacie. "Let's get out of here."

"Agreed. Let them be stupid. We don't have to be." Jacie turned her horse back the way they'd come and had taken the lead when the sharp report of gunfire echoed off the canyon walls.

"What the hell?" Jacie's horse spun beneath her and it was all she could do to keep her balance.

Aramis reared. Tracie planted her feet hard in the stirrups and leaned forward, holding on until the gelding dropped to all four hooves.

More gunfire ensued, followed by the pounding of hooves, the sound growing louder as it neared them.

Tracie yelled, "Go, Jacie. Get out of the canyon!"

Jacie didn't hesitate, nor did her horse. She dug her heals into D'Artagnan's flanks, sending him flying along the trail. She headed back the way they'd come, her horse skimming over the rocky ground, his head stretched forward, nostrils flared.

Before they'd gone a hundred yards, Rocky, the gelding Mr. Jones had been riding, raced past them, eyes wide, sweat lathered on both sides, sporting an empty saddle, no Mr. Jones. Rocky hit the trailhead leading out of the canyon, scrambling up the slope.

Jacie dared to glance over her shoulder.

Mr. Smith emerged from the fork in the canyon trail, yelling at Ginger, kicking her hard. Both leaned forward, racing for their lives.

The distinct sound of revving motors chased the horse and rider through the narrow passage. An ATV roared into the open, followed by another, then another until four ATVs spread out, chasing Mr. Smith, Tracie and Jacie.

Jacie reached the trail climbing out of the canyon first, urging D'Artagnan faster. He stumbled, regained his footing and charged on.

Tracie wasn't far behind, her horse equally determined to make it out of the canyon alive and ahead of the ATVs.

Mr. Smith brought up the rear on Ginger.

As Jacie reached the top of the slope, she turned back, praying for Tracie to hurry.

Her sister had dropped behind, Aramis slipping in the loose rocks and gravel, distressed by the noise behind him. Just when Jacie thought the two were going to make it, shots rang out from the base of the canyon.

One of the ATVs had stopped, its rider aiming what appeared to be a high-powered rifle with a scope up at the riders on the trail.

Another shot rang out and Mr. Smith jerked in his saddle and fell off backward, sliding down the hill on his back.

His mount screamed and surged up the narrow trail past Tracie and Aramis.

Three of the ATVs raced up the path, bumping and slipping over the loose rocks.

From her vantage point at the top of the ridge, Jacie stood helpless as the horror unfolded.

Aramis reared, dumping Tracie off his back.

She hit the ground and rolled, sliding down the slope back toward the base of the canyon.

Jacie yanked her rifle from its scabbard, slid out of her saddle and dropped to a kneeling position, aiming at the man at the base of the canyon.

The man was aiming at her.

Jacie held her breath, lined up the sights and pulled the trigger a second before he fired his gun.

His bullet hit the ground at her feet, kicking up dirt into her eyes.

For a second she couldn't see, but when her vision cleared, she saw the man she'd aimed for lay on the ground beside his ATV, struggling to get up.

One down, three to go.

Ginger topped the rise, followed by Aramis, spooking D'Artagnan. He pulled against the reins Jacie held on to tightly. She didn't let go, but she couldn't get another round off while he jerked her around.

When he settled, she aimed at the closest rider to her. He was halfway up the hill, headed straight for her.

She popped off a round, nicked him in the shoulder, sending him flying off the vehicle. The ATV slipped over the edge of the trail and tumbled to the bottom.

The other two riders were on their way up the hill. One split off and headed back down the side, straight for where Tracie lay sprawled against the slope, low crawling for her Glock that had slipped loose of its holster. The other rider raced toward Jacie.

Jacie aimed at the man headed for Tracie.

D'Artagnan pulled against the reins, sending Jacie's bullet flying wide of its target.

She didn't have time to adjust her aim for the rider nearing the top of the hill. He was too close and coming too fast.

Jacie let go of D'Artagnan's reins, flipped her rifle around and swung just as the rider topped the hill. She caught him in the chest with all the force of her swing and his upward movement. Jacie reeled backward landing hard on her butt, the wind knocked out of her.

The rider flew off the back of the vehicle and tumbled over the ridge.

Jacie scrambled to the edge and watched as the rider cartwheeled down the steep slope, over and over until he came to a crumpled stop, midway down.

The last rider standing had reached Tracie before she could get to her gun. He gathered her in his arms and stuck a pistol to her head. *"Pare o dispararé a mujer!"*

Even if she couldn't understand his demand, Jacie got the message. If she didn't stop, he'd shoot her sister.

Two more ATVs arrived on the canyon floor.

Jacie had no choice. She didn't want to leave her sister in the hands of the thugs below, but she couldn't fight them when they held the trump card—her sister.

She eased away from the edge of the ridge and scoped her options.

D'Artagnan and the other horses were long gone, headed back to the safety of the Big Elk Ranch barn.

The ATV she'd knocked the rider off stood near the edge of the ridge. If she hoped to escape, she had to make a run for it.

Jacie ducked low and ran for the ATV, jumped onto the seat, pulled the crank cord and held her breath.

The two new ATV riders were on their way up the hill. The man holding Tracie fired off a shot, but his pistol's range wasn't good enough to be accurate at that distance.

The ATV engine turned over and died.

Jacie pulled the cord again and the engine roared to life. She gave the vehicle gas and leaped forward, speeding toward the closest help she could find. The Raging Bull Ranch.

She had a good head start on the other two, but they didn't have to know where they were going; they only had to follow.

Jacie ripped the throttle wide open, bouncing

hard over obstacles she could barely see in the failing light.

The sun had completely dipped below the horizon, the gray of dusk slipping over the land like a shroud. Until all the stars twinkled to life, Jacie could only hope she was headed in the right direction.

After thirty minutes of full-out racing across cactus, dodging clumps of saw palmetto, lights appeared ahead. Her heartbeat fluttered and tears threatened to blind her as she skidded up to a gate. She flung herself off the bike and fell to the ground, her legs shaking too badly to hold her up.

Dragging herself to her feet, she unlatched the gate and ran toward the house. "Help! Help! Please, dear God, help!"

As she neared the huge house, a shadow detached itself from the porch and ran toward her.

On her last leg, her strength giving out, Jacie flung herself into the man's arms. "Please help me."

Chapter Two

Zach staggered back, the force with which the woman with the long brown ponytail hit him knocking him back several steps before he could get his balance. He wrapped his arm around her automatically, steadying her as her knees buckled and she slipped toward the floor.

"Please help me," she sobbed.

"What's wrong?" He scooped her into his arms and carried her through the open French doors into his bedroom and laid her on the bed.

Boots clattered on the wooden slats of the porch and more came running down the hallway. Two of Hank's security guards burst into Zach's room through the French doors at the same time Hank entered from the hallway.

The security guards stood with guns drawn, their black-clad bodies looking more like ninjas than billionaire bodyguards.

"It's okay, I have everything under control," Zach said. Though he doubted seriously he had anything under control. He had no idea who this woman was or what she'd meant by *help me.*

Hank burst through the bedroom door, his face drawn in tense lines. "What's going on? I heard the sound of an engine outside and shouting coming from this side of the house." He glanced at Zach's bed and the woman stirring against the comforter. "What do we have here?"

She pushed to a sitting position and blinked up at Zach. "Where am I?"

"You're on the Raging Bull Ranch."

"Oh, dear God." She pushed to the edge of the bed and tried to stand. "I have to get back. They have her. Oh, sweet Jesus, they have Tracie."

Zach slipped an arm around her waist and pulled her to him to keep her from falling flat on her face again. "Where do you have to get back to? And who's Tracie?"

"Tracie's my twin. We were leading a hunting party on the Big Elk. They shot, she fell, now they have her." The woman grabbed Zach's shirt with both fists. "You have to help her."

"You're not making sense. Slow down, take a deep breath and start over."

"We don't have time!" The woman pushed away from Zach and raced for the French doors. "We have to get back before they kill her." She stumbled over a throw rug and hit the hardwood floor on her knees. "I shouldn't have left her." She buried her face in her hands and sobbed.

Zach stared at the woman, a flash of memory anchoring his feet to the floor. He remembered his partner, Antoinette Gutierrez—Toni—in a similar position, her face battered, her hair matted with her own blood, begging for her life.

The room spun around him, the air growing thick, hard to breathe.

Not until Hank ran forward and helped the woman to her feet did Zach snap out of it.

"We'll help," Hank promised. "Where is your sister?"

The woman looked up and blinked the tears from her eyes, her shoulders straightening. "Wild Horse Canyon."

"Joe." Hank addressed one of his bodyguards. "Wake the foreman and tell him we need all the four-wheelers gassed up and ready to go immediately."

Joe jammed his weapon into his shoulder holster and ran out the open French doors.

Hank turned to the other bodyguard. "Max, grab the first aid supplies from the pantry, along with one of the blankets kept in the hall closet. Meet us at the barn in two minutes."

"A woman needs our help." Hank turned to Zach. "Are you coming or not?"

The woman in question's eyes narrowed as

she stared from Hank to Zach. "I don't care who comes, but we need to get there fast. If they take her hostage, the longer we wait, the harder it will be to find them."

"Understood."

Zach stared at the woman, his pulse pounding against his eardrums, his palms damp and clammy. "I'll come." The words echoed in the room, bouncing off the walls to hit him square in the gut. He'd committed to helping an unknown woman when he'd failed to help the partner he'd been with for three years.

Hank steered the woman toward Zach. "Find out what you can while I call the sheriff and let him know what's going on."

When Hank left the room, the woman glanced at Zach. "Are you coming or not?"

Having committed to the task at hand, Zach hooked the woman's arm, ready to get the job over with as quickly as possible. "It would help if we knew who you are."

"Jacie Kosart. I work on the Big Elk Ranch. It's a three-hundred-fifty-thousand-acre spread bordering the Raging Bull and the Big Bend National Park."

"Jacie." He rolled the name on his tongue for a second, then dove in. "What were you doing out this late?"

"My sister and I were leading a big-game hunting party for my boss, Richard Giddings. The two men who'd commissioned us didn't want to hunt on the normal trails the deer like to travel." Jacie explained how they'd come to the canyon, the subsequent shootings and her escape. "We have to get back. I think they killed the two hunters. If not, they need medical help." She gulped, tears welling again. "Tracie has to be all right. She just has to."

"We'll do the best we can to find her and bring her home." Zach tried to sound confident when he felt nothing like it. If the men in the canyon had anything to do with the drug cartels, Jacie's sister was as good as dead.

The sound of engines revving outside signaled the end of their conversation and the need to move.

Zach cupped Jacie's elbow and led her through the French doors and out to the barn where five ATVs idled in neutral. The man Zach assumed was Hank's foreman sat astride one of them giving the engine gas.

Hank, dressed in jeans, a denim jacket and cowboy boots, jogged down from the house flanked by his two bodyguards, each carrying an automatic assault weapon. Hank carried two, one of which he tossed to Zach. "In case we run into some trouble."

Zach dropped his hold on the woman's arm and

caught the high-powered weapon, slipping it into the scabbard on one of the four-wheelers.

"You all right?" he asked Jacie.

She nodded. "Yeah. I just want to find my sister."

The two bodyguards mounted a four-wheeler each and Hank took another, leaving only one left.

"The girl can ride with you. I don't want her falling off and injuring herself. This way you can keep an eye on her and lead the way."

Zach frowned but mounted the ATV and scooted forward for Jacie to climb on the back.

She balked, staring at Zach and the space allotted to her. "I can take the one I rode in on."

"We don't know how much gas it has in it, and given that you've passed out once, you're better off riding with one of us."

Zach sucked in a deep breath and let it out. "Get on."

Jacie flung her leg over the back and slid in behind Zach, her thighs resting against his, her chest pressing into his back.

He revved the engine and shot out of the barnyard headed south.

With Jacie looking over his shoulder, directing him, he raced across the dark earth, dodging clumps of prickly pear cactus and saw palmettos.

The woman held on lightly at first, her grip tightening as Zach swerved in and out of the vegetation with nothing but the stars shining down on him from a moonless sky.

As they neared the edge of the canyon, Jacie pointed and yelled over the roar of the engine. "There!"

Zach pulled up short of the edge of the canyon. On the slim chance the assailants were hanging around at the bottom of the canyon, he didn't want to provide them with a target at the top. He cut the engine.

Before he could dismount, Jacie was off the back and scrambling toward the edge.

He caught her as she lunged for the trail, yanking her back from the edge and out of line of sight from the bottom. "Are you trying to get yourself killed?"

"My sister was down there. We have to save her." She struggled against his hold.

"For all we know they could still be down there."

She fought to free her arm. "Then let's go."

The other riders had pulled to a halt and dismounted.

Zach dragged Jacie over to Hank. "Hold on to her while I check it out."

"Take Joe with you in case you run into trouble."

"I do better on my own." Zach crouched low and dropped over the rim of the canyon, slipping down the trail as quietly as possible. In the light from the night sky, he could make out where the trail was disturbed, one edge knocked free. Probably where a horse, a motorcycle or a four-wheeler had run off the side.

The bottom of the trail was bathed in shadows, making it hard to distinguish the boulders from crouching thugs waiting to pounce.

Careful not to fall off the edge himself, Zach moved swiftly down the trail, reaching the bottom. The shadows proved to be boulders and one wrecked ATV, crumpled among them. Nothing moved. Zach explored among the boulders to the other side of the ATV and found the body of a man laying at an awkward angle, facedown, his leg bent, probably shattered in the fall. The ground beside him sported an inky-black stain.

Zach didn't have to guess that the stain was a drying pool of this man's blood. This guy hadn't died from the fall, based on the dark bullet-sized circle in the middle of his back. If Zach turned him over, he'd likely be a mess on the other side where the bullet exited his body.

Zach searched the area around the base of the cliff and shouted up, "Clear!"

Five four-wheelers inched down the narrow trail, lights picking out the way.

Joe led the pack followed by Hank, Max, the foreman and Jacie.

Zach frowned and met her as she cleared the trail. "You should have stayed at the top."

"Did you find her?" Jacie glanced around, her eyes wide, hopeful. Then her shoulders sagged and she slumped on the seat of the ATV. "That's Mr. Smith, one of the two hunters we were escorting." She sucked in a deep breath and let it out slowly. "Tracie's not here, is she?"

"Believe it or not, that's a good thing." Hank left his four-wheeler and crossed to Jacie. "If she's not here, it's a good chance that she's still alive."

Jacie's jaw tightened. "Then come on, let's find her."

Zach shook his head. "It would be suicide to continue searching in the dark. If the attackers are in the canyon still, they would have the advantage and pick us off from above."

"We can't leave her out there."

"Zach's right. We have to wait until daylight." Hank stood beside Zach. "Going in at night wouldn't be doing your sister any favors."

"Then I'll go on alone." As she pressed the gas lever, Zach grabbed her around the waist and yanked her off the bike.

"You're not going anywhere." Zach slammed her against his chest, his arms wrapping around her waist. "One captive is enough. We don't want to risk another. Besides, your sister most likely wouldn't want you to risk it."

Jacie struggled against him. "Let go of me. My sister is my responsibility."

"Then take your responsibility seriously and do what's smart. We need to wait until daylight before we risk going into that canyon."

The woman stopped. "I guess you're right."

When she quit struggling and seemed to settle down, Zach released her. In the next second, she shot across to the four-wheeler she'd left running, hopped on and took off on the trail leading into the canyon.

"Damn, woman." Zach ran after her, catching up as she entered the narrow trail flanked by high cliffs.

As she slowed to negotiate around a boulder, Zach jogged alongside her and jumped on the back. "Stop, damn it!"

"Not until I find my sister." She goosed the accelerator lever on the handle and nearly unseated him.

Zach grabbed around her middle and held on.

They slid around a corner, the starlight barely reaching them at this point.

About the time Zach steadied himself, Jacie hit the brakes and jerked the handles, sending the machine sliding sideways, and the tail end with Zach slipping around to the right.

JACIE COULDN'T LET the search end. Not when her sister's life hung in the balance.

When she saw the cowboy boot, she slammed on her brakes. In a random patch of starlight, a jean-clad leg peeked out from behind a large boulder.

Her heart skipped several beats and then hammered against the wall of her chest. Jacie threw herself off the four-wheeler and scrambled up from her hands and knees to run toward the leg, sobs rising from her throat, echoing off the canyon walls.

Footsteps crunched behind her. Probably Zach, but she didn't care. If this was Tracie... *Oh, dear God, please be okay.*

The other four-wheelers entered the canyon at a more moderate pace, coming to a halt behind Jacie's.

She dropped to her knees beside a body, relief washing over her as soon as she saw it was a man.

"It's Mr. Jones." She felt for a pulse, her hand still for a long time before she glanced back at Zach, a glimmer of hope daring to make an appearance. "I have a pulse. It's weak, but I have a pulse." She leaned into the man's face. "Mr. Jones, can you hear me?"

Nothing. Her hopes dying, she tried again, patting the man's cheek gently. "Mr. Jones, please. Can you hear me?"

A muscle twitched in the man's leg.

Encouraged, Jacie spoke louder. "Mr. Jones, we're going to get you some help, but can you help us?"

The man's eyes fluttered open. "Set…up." He closed his eyes again.

"Mr. Jones!" Jacie wanted to shake the man but was afraid to add to his injuries. "Please, did you see where they went? Where did they take my sister?"

His eyes never opened, but his lips moved.

Jacie leaned in closer, tilting her head to hear what he whispered.

"Not Jones."

Jacie leaned back. "What do you mean?"

The man whispered again.

Leaning close, Jacie caught what sounded like letters.

"D…E…A." As if it had taken everything he had left, the last letter ended on a raspy exhale.

Mr. Jones, or whoever he was, didn't draw another breath.

Jacie felt for a pulse. Not even a weak one thumped against her fingertips. "No pulse. He's not breathing." She clamped his nose with her fingers and breathed for him.

Zach dropped to his knees on the other side of him and leaned the heel of his palms into the man's chest five times. "Now breathe," he instructed.

Jacie blew into the man's mouth. His lungs expanded, pushing his chest up.

Zach resumed his compressions. For every five, Jacie breathed one breath.

Hank and the bodyguards scoured the vicinity while Zach and Jacie worked over Mr. Jones.

When they returned, Jacie glanced up at Hank. "Any sign of my sister?" She knew the answer, but she had to ask.

"None."

Rather than let the news cripple her, Jacie renewed her efforts to save Mr. Jones.

After fifteen minutes, Zach quit pumping the man's chest and he touched Jacie's arm before she could breathe into the man's mouth.

"He's gone."

"No." Jacie sat back on her haunches. "He might have told us where they went."

"I doubt it. From what you said, he was hit before they grabbed Tracie." Zach rose to his feet and held out a hand to Jacie. "Come on, let's get you back to the ranch. We'll start the search in the morning."

"She has to be okay." Jacie let him pull her to her feet, where she leaned against him, pressing her forehead against the solid wall of his chest. "She's all I have."

Hank patted her back. "We'll find her. Don't you worry."

Zach stood beside her. "I saw his lips moving, but I couldn't hear him. What did Jones say to you before he died?"

"I'm not sure." Jacie shook her head. She'd never had someone die on her. Hell, she'd never seen someone get shot in all the years she'd been working on the Big Elk Ranch. She'd never seen someone die of a gunshot wound. She pushed the image of the dead men from her mind and concentrated on the only clue she might have to find her sister. "At first he said what sounded like 'set… up.' Then he said 'Not Jones…D…E…A.'"

Zach stiffened against her, his hands gripping her arm. "Are you sure?"

She glanced up into his face. "As sure as I can be. The man was barely able to whisper. I could have gotten it wrong. Why?"

"Damn. These men most likely were agents with the DEA."

Hank ran a hand through his shocking-white hair and looked around the canyon walls. "Think they were set up?"

"Sounds like it."

Jacie froze. "Oh, dear God." She didn't, she couldn't have… "My sister is an FBI agent here on vacation to visit me."

Zach still held her.

Jacie was sure, if he weren't still gripping her

arms, she'd have fallen to her knees. "Do you think she was working undercover, as well?"

"If so, and it was a setup…" Zach's jaw tightened. "Apparently, there's some bad blood in both agencies."

Hank sighed. "Holy hell. I was too late, then."

Zach dropped his hold on Jacie. "What do you mean?"

"I'm sorry, Jacie. I've failed your sister." Hank reached out for one of Jacie's hands. "You see, Tracie came to me yesterday asking for my help."

"I don't understand." Jacie's head spun. Had she been walking around in the clouds since her sister arrived? "My sister only got here two days ago. Why would she come to you?"

"She wanted help finding out who was the leak in her agency and she didn't want to go through official channels." Hank's gaze shifted back to Zach. "Since you are former FBI, this was to be your first assignment."

Chapter Three

Zach rode back to the Raging Bull Ranch, a knot the size of Texas twisting his gut.

Hank couldn't be serious. To ask him to take on the FBI as his first assignment? The organization that had left him and Toni to die in the godforsaken hell of the Los Lobos cartel in the Mexican state of Chihuahua?

Captured in Juarez on assignment, drugged and transported to a squalid compound in Mexico, Zach and Toni had been tortured and starved in the cartel's attempt to attain information from them about who in the FBI was supplying military weapons to their archrivals, La Familia Diablos.

He'd been forced to watch as they raped, mutilated and finally killed Toni. Bound and gagged, he'd been helpless, unable to do anything to save her.

When another gang stormed the compound, they'd crashed into the concrete building where Zach had been held, giving him the opportunity to escape under cover of the night. But it had been too late for Toni.

Wounded, dehydrated and barely able to see through swollen eyes, he dragged himself out of the compound and hid in the mountains, stealing food from a farmer until he could make his way back to the States.

Two years, surgery, rehab and psychiatric treatment had healed the external scars, but the internal ones festered like a disease.

Jacie rode on the back of the four-wheeler, her arms circled around Zach's waist.

Hank wanted him to help her and her sister, who was certain to be experiencing exactly what Toni had been subjected to, if not worse. If she wasn't dead, likely she would be wishing she was soon.

No. Zach couldn't do this. He couldn't commit to finding Tracie, not when he knew the outcome wouldn't be good. Her twin would expect him to come back with a woman intact, healthy and cared for.

The arms around him tightened, reminding him that the woman on the back of the vehicle was already counting on him to help her.

As he pulled into the barnyard of the Raging Bull Ranch, he mentally prepared his exit speech. "Hank, I'd like to talk with you privately."

No use bringing the woman in on his cowardly

departure. She wouldn't understand, and seeing the desperation in her eyes would only drive another stake through his heart.

Red and blue flashing lights shone from the road leading into the Raging Bull Ranch.

"Zach, we'll talk as soon as I've had a chance to bring the local law enforcement up to date on the situation. Meet me in my office in five minutes." Hank and his two bodyguards left. The foreman rode one of the four-wheelers to the back of the barn, leaving Zach alone with Jacie.

He glanced away from her, the look of worry and sadness in her eyes more than he could handle.

A hand on his arm precluded ignoring the woman. "Zach, what are we going to do now? How are we going to find my sister?"

"There is no *we*." His words came out sharper than he'd intended.

Jacie snatched her hand away from his arm as if she'd been bitten. "What do you mean? I thought Hank said you were the one assigned to help Tracie."

"If I chose to accept the assignment and go to work for Hank in his insane business." Zach snorted. "Truth and justice. There is no truth and justice when a gun's held to your head or a whip's lashed across your naked skin. I won't be a part of Hank's fantasy."

"You mean you're going to turn your back on my sister and leave her to die?"

Her words struck him where it hurt most. Square in his gut where guilt ate away at his insides. "I can't do anything for your sister." He turned his back to her. "She's as good as dead."

"No! She's alive. She's my twin. I can feel her presence." Jacie grabbed his arm and jerked him around. "You can't just walk away. My sister needs you. I need you. I can't do this on my own. I will if I have to. But I wouldn't know where to start."

"Don't worry, Hank will find some other cowboy to ride to your rescue. It just won't be me. I'm not the right man for this job."

"You're not a man at all," Jacie spat out. "What kind of man would run away rather than help save a woman's life?"

Zach rounded on her and grabbed her arms in a vicious grip. His heart slammed against his ribs, and rage rose up his neck to explode in his head. "That's right! I *can't* help your sister. I *can't* save a woman from the cartel. I couldn't save Toni and I refuse to watch it happen all over again. I. Can't. Help. *Got that?*" He shook her hard.

Tears welled in Jacie's gray-blue eyes, her long, rich brown hair falling down over her face. "I get it. You have your own issues. Fine. I'll do this without you." She struggled against his hold. "Let go of me. I don't want or need you or any of Hank's hired guns. I'll get my sister back. Alive! Mark my words." She shook free of him. "In the meantime go find a bottle to crawl into or see a shrink. Whatever. I don't give a damn." She spun on her booted heels and marched away from him.

The farther away she moved, the more Zach's chest tightened. If Jacie went tearing off after her sister, she'd end up captured and tortured, as well. What kind of fool would throw herself at the cartel and expect to survive?

The rage subsided, leaving Zach cold and empty.

Jacie was a fool. But she was a fool who loved her sister enough to sacrifice her life to save her twin.

Zach had begged his captors to torture him and leave his partner alone. Instead they'd tortured her in their efforts to drag information out of *him*. Sadly he didn't have the information they'd wanted and Toni had paid the price for his ignorance. His captors had wanted the name of the agent feeding their rivals information about upcoming sting operations. While the Los Lobos cartel took hits, losing some of their best contacts, La Familia Diablos got away with all their people and goods intact.

Heartsick by his own agency's betrayal, Zach had returned to the States, healed his wounds and quit the FBI. Tired of the politics, the graft and corruption.

If Tracie had been after the same person...the one disloyal to his country and fellow agents... she was crazy. The traitor kept his hand so close to his chest. No one knew who he was.

As Jacie disappeared around the corner of the ranch house, Zach started after her. Jacie, unskilled in the art of spying and tactics, wouldn't last two minutes going up against a drug cartel.

His footsteps sped up until he was jogging. Since he was on the outside looking in, he might discover who the mole was in the FBI, the man who'd sacrificed his own people to line his pockets with blood money.

Jacie had almost reached Hank when Zach caught up with her. "Wait."

The woman kept walking. "Why should I? I told you, I don't need you or anyone else to help me find my sister."

He snagged her arm and spun her toward him. "Look. Despite what you're saying, you won't last two minutes out there. The cartel employs trained killers. What kind of training have you had in shooting and dodging bullets?"

Her shoulders were thrown back, her chin held high. "I'm a damned good shot."

"At game. Ever shot a person?"

Her eyes narrowed. "Not before tonight."

"You have to be willing to shoot before you're shot."

"I'll do whatever it takes to find my sister and bring her back alive." She swallowed hard, her chin rising even higher. "Even if it means killing a man to do it. And I might just start with you if you don't let go of me."

He dropped his hold. "You were also right that I have issues. I won't go into it, but they involved the cartel. I've been on both sides of the border. I know what to expect."

"So? You just said you wouldn't help me."

He sucked in a breath and let it out slowly before capturing her gaze with a steady one of his own. "Though I think the effort is futile, I'll help you find your sister."

Jacie snorted. "No, thanks." She turned away and would have walked off.

Zach grabbed her hand and steeled himself to reveal a piece of his soul he hadn't revealed to anyone. "I watched someone I cared for tortured and killed by the Los Lobos Cartel. It's not something I want to do again. I promise to do my best to find your sister before she meets the same fate."

Jacie's eyes flared wide, then narrowed again. "How do I know you won't flip out on me again?"

"I'm a good agent." He paused. "I *was* a good

agent. I know when to focus and I'm driven to get the job done."

"Then why did you quit the FBI?"

"For the same reason your sister asked for help from Hank. I was betrayed by someone on the inside. My partner paid with blood. If I can find your sister and, in the process, find the mole, my partner will not have died in vain."

Jacie's eyes narrowed even more and she chewed on her bottom lip. Finally she stuck out her hand. "Okay, then. Let's go find my sister."

JACIE SHOOK ZACH'S hand, her fingers tingling where they touched his. She wasn't completely convinced Zach was her man, and she didn't like the way her pulse quickened when he was near, but she didn't have a whole lot of choices. Going searching for the people responsible for her sister's abduction would be hard enough on her own.... Hell, it would be impossible. Having a former FBI agent on her side would be a step in the right direction. He might still have connections and contacts.

Hank led the county sheriff over to join them. "Zach, this is Sheriff Fulmer from Wild Oak Canyon. He'll be working with the FBI and DEA on this case."

Zach shook the sheriff's hand.

Jacie refused to, knowing the man's track record

since he'd taken office a year ago. He tended to look the other way rather than stop the flow of drugs through his county. "When will the DEA and FBI be sending someone out to assist?" And hopefully take over the operation.

"I spoke to the regional director of the FBI a few minutes ago. They're as concerned as you are to get your sister back. As for the DEA agents, the county coroner and the state crime lab are on their way out as we speak. If you could show me where the bodies are, I'll cordon off the crime scene until they arrive."

"My foreman will take you out there," Hank said. "If I need to sign any statements, let me know."

"From what Mr. Derringer says, I'll need a full statement from you, Ms. Kosart, as you're the only eyewitness."

"I'll provide one in the morning. Right now I need to get back to the Big Elk Ranch and notify my employer of the situation and check on the horses." She hadn't even thought once about the horses since Tracie had been taken. Now she focused on them to keep from going crazy with inaction.

"I'm going with you." Zach glanced at Hank. "I'm in."

Hank nodded, ignoring the raised eyebrows of the sheriff. "Keep me informed, will ya?" was all he said; then he turned his attention to the sheriff. "Scott, my foreman, and I will show you where we found the two agents." He led the officer away.

"Give me a minute while I get my keys." Zach pointed toward a black four-wheel-drive pickup standing in the circular drive. "You can wait by my truck."

"Okay, but hurry. I'm worried about the horses." Jacie was worried about a lot more than just the horses, but she trudged toward the vehicle, taking her time, while Zach ducked into the ranch house.

Jacie recognized the truck as a model produced a couple of years before. It wasn't new, but it shone like a new truck with only a thin layer of dust coating the shiny wax finish. The man had some issues, but taking care of what was his wasn't one of them.

He returned in two minutes, carrying a small duffel bag in one hand, wearing a black cowboy hat and a light leather jacket. When it flapped open, the black leather of a shoulder holster was revealed with a pistol nestled inside.

Jacie had spent her life around men and guns, working for the Big Elk Ranch. Leading hunting parties required a thorough knowledge of how to shoot, clean and unjam weapons of all shapes and sizes. Knowing Zach carried a pistol and was former FBI gave her a small sense of comfort that she wasn't the only one who could handle a gun going forward in the search for her sister.

Before he reached her he clicked the door lock release.

Jacie climbed into the truck and buckled herself into the passenger seat.

Zach stashed the bag in the backseat and settled behind the steering wheel. "You'll have to tell me where to go. I'm new around here."

She gave him the directions and sat back, staring ahead where the headlights illuminated the road, keeping an eye out for the wildlife that skirted the shoulders looking for something to eat. Too many times she'd had near misses with the local deer.

In her peripheral vision, she watched the way Zach handled the truck with ease, his fingers gripping the steering wheel a little tighter than necessary, his face set in grim lines. She wanted to know more about him; what made his eyes so dark and caused the shadows beneath? Had his experience with the cartel left such an indelible mark he couldn't separate that chapter of his life with a possible future?

"Toni was your partner?" she asked.

The fingers on the steering wheel tightened until the knuckles turned white. For a long moment Zach didn't answer.

About the time Jacie gave up on getting a response, he spoke.

"Yes, Toni was my partner."

"I'm sorry. You two must have been close." Jacie dragged her gaze from the pain reflected from his eyes. "Did he leave behind a family?"

"*She* wasn't married. Her father was her only relative."

Interesting. So his partner had been female. Which would explain his reluctance to go after another female when he'd failed the first. Jacie chewed on that bit of information. "Were you in love with her?"

As soon as the question left her lips, Jacie could have smacked herself. The man was torn up enough about losing his partner. Bringing it up had to be killing him. Her curiosity didn't warrant grilling him about his past. "I'm sorry, this must be painful. I'll shut up."

"Yes."

"Yes that you want me to shut up or yes that you loved her?"

His lips twitched, the movement softening his features to almost human. "Both."

Jacie sat back, her gaze back on the road, her chest tightening. "Turn left at the next road."

Zach nodded.

"Did she know you loved her?" Jacie closed her eyes. "That was too personal. You don't have to answer. I'm sorry. While Tracie went into the FBI, I knew I couldn't because I can't keep my mouth shut unless I'm out hunting."

"Pretend you're hunting." Zach turned where she'd indicated. "And no. She didn't know." He pulled up to a closed gate attached to six-foot-high fencing. "Game ranch?"

"That's what I do. I didn't go to Quantico or study to be a doctor. I got my marketing degree from the University of Texas and came back here to work as a hunting party coordinator, a fancy title for trail guide. It allows me to be where I love to be, outside, and working with horses and people." She couldn't help the defensive tone in her voice.

"I'm not judging."

"I love my sister and I'm so proud of her, but part of me feels as though I didn't push hard enough, that I'm not living up to my potential. I went on trail rides while my sister ran off to be an FBI agent working for the good of her country."

"And look what it got her." Zach's lips thinned. "Betrayal by that country she's fighting for."

"I don't believe that. One bad apple, and all that, doesn't mean everyone will turn traitor. I still believe in the FBI and the other branches of service dedicated to protecting our freedom. And I'm sure Tracie feels the same. If she knew there was a mole in the organization, she didn't run from it, she went looking for it. Especially since she asked Hank for help."

Zach nodded toward the gate. "I take it the gate doesn't open without a remote."

Jacie's face heated. She slipped from the truck and ran to the gate, punching in a code, triggering the automatic gate opener arm to swing out.

Jacie climbed back into the truck and sat quietly as Zach drove the winding road that led to the lodge at the Big Elk Ranch.

The lights shone bright, unusual for the earliest hours of the morning.

Before the vehicle came to a halt, Richard Giddings leaped off the porch and opened the passenger door to the pickup. "Oh, thank God." The tall man with the slightly graying temples reached out. His hands circled her waist and he lifted Jacie to the ground. "I'd been so worried about you. When your hunting party never returned, I had everyone out looking until midnight. When Derringer called to say you were on your way, I was relieved and sick all at once." He wrapped an arm around her shoulder and led her toward the house. He'd taken a couple of steps before he stopped and stared down into her eyes. "I'm so sorry about your sister."

Despite the exhaustion threatening to overwhelm her, Jacie planted her feet in the ground and threw back her shoulders. "Tracie will be all right. We'll get her back."

Richard smiled down at her with his warm green eyes. "She's a fighter, just like her sister."

"Damn right." Jacie backed away from her boss. "Richard, I'd like you to meet Zach." She stopped, realizing for the first time she didn't know Zach's full name. She tilted her head and raised her eyebrows, hoping he'd take the hint.

Zach stepped forward and held out his hand. "Zach Adams."

Richard's eyebrows V'd over his nose. "Should I know you?"

"Not at all." He glanced at Jacie and smiled. "Jacie and I go way back to college, don't we?"

"Y-yes. We do."

"We dated for a while, lost touch, but I just couldn't forget her. And since I was in the neighborhood, I planned on reconnecting in the morning, once I got my bearings." He shook his head. "Imagine my surprise when she found me first at Hank's place."

Richard held out a hand and shook Zach's. "You picked a really bad time."

"No, actually." Jacie crossed to Zach's side. "I'm glad he's here. With Tracie being gone and all, it's nice to have the support of…friends." She hooked her arm through his. "Do you mind if he stays in the Javelina Cabin? I know it's empty."

And it was the closest one to the tiny cabin she'd called home since she came to work full-time at the Big Elk Ranch.

"Sure." Richard nodded. "You can show him the way. I'll have Tia Fuentez make up a plate of food since you missed dinner. How about you, Mr. Adams? Hungry?"

"Call me Zach. And no, thank you. I had my supper." He pulled Jacie close. "But I'll use that time to get a shower and hit the rack."

"Make yourself at home. The ranch is big, but the people are friendly."

"I've noticed that." He smiled again at Jacie. "I'm looking forward to catching up with Jacie, and maybe we'll hear something about her sister soon."

Jacie steered Zach toward the line of cabins leading away from the lodge. As soon as they were out of listening range, she whispered, "Why did you lie to my boss?"

"I'd just as soon everyone in this part of Texas think that I'm here as an old college buddy or boyfriend, rather than an agent searching for your sister. In this case, we don't know who are the good guys and who are the bad guys. So we play it neutral and I blend in. The best undercover agents are those who blend in."

"Okay, then. When do we start looking for my sister?"

"Was that a helicopter I saw out by the barn?"

Jacie frowned, taken off guard by the change in subject. "Yes, Richard has a helicopter he uses occasionally for the big game hunts or flight-seeing tours over Big Bend."

"Think he'll take us up so that we can fly over the canyon?"

Her heart fluttered with excitement. "I'm sure he will. I'll ask." Maybe they'd spot the people holding Tracie.

"Good. It would be better coming from you, since it's your sister and you work here. Remember, I'm just a boyfriend."

Her cheeks warmed at the thought of Zach as her boyfriend, even if it was pretend. "I'll get right on it."

"I'm gonna hit the sack for a few hours of sleep. We have a busy day ahead of us. I suggest you do the same."

She nodded, staring out at the night sky, wondering what her sister was going through and if she was okay. "We're going to find her."

When he didn't respond, Jacie's fists tightened. "We *will* find my sister."

"I promise you this." He faced her, capturing her cheeks in his hands, his gaze severe, his lips pressed into a firm line. "I'll do the best I can."

A shiver rippled across Jacie's skin as she gazed into his brown-black eyes. The intensity of his stare and the tightness of his grip on her face gave her a sense of comfort and commitment. This man had lost someone he loved to terrorist cartel members. He wouldn't let it happen again if he could help it. They would get her sister back or die trying.

Chapter Four

Jacie showed Zach to the cabin and left him to get a shower.

After retrieving his duffel bag, he checked his cell phone, surprised that he had reception. Out in the boonies of south Texas, he hadn't seen much in the way of reception outside the small town of Wild Oak Canyon. The Big Elk Ranch must have a cell tower of its own.

Glad for the ability to use his own phone, Zach didn't lose time in contacting an old buddy from his Quantico days back on the East Coast.

"Hello?" a gravelly voice answered on the fifth ring.

"Jim, Zach Adams."

"Zach?" James Coslowski paused. The sound of something falling in the background, followed by a curse, crossed the airwaves. "Do you realize it's only three in the morning?"

"Sorry for the late call, but I need a favor."

"And it couldn't have waited until morning?"

"No. I need to know everything about Special Agent Tracie Kosart that you can find, and as soon as possible."

"I repeat…this couldn't wait until I've had a gallon of coffee, say after a more reasonable hour like seven?"

"She was abducted tonight by what appears to be a Mexican drug cartel."

"Damn." The gravel had been scraped from Jim's voice. "You know I'm not supposed to release any information—"

"I know. I'm asking as a huge favor. I'm working this case as a private investigator, but I need to know why they would have abducted her. Anything you can find out and share would help."

"Still, you're no longer with the agency."

Zach snorted. "Since when are you a rule follower?"

"Since I got married and have a wife, and a baby on the way."

Zach's chest tightened. "Sorry, man. I didn't know. Congratulations."

"There's a lot you don't know, having dropped off the face of the earth for the past two years." Jim sighed. "I'll do the best I can. Just don't go all vigilante and get yourself into trouble."

Zach's fist tightened around the cell phone. "What difference would it make? I didn't get any help from my employer last time. I certainly don't expect any better this time."

"Just stay safe. Some of us care what happens to you."

His heart pounding against his ribs, Zach ended the call, grabbed a towel from the bathroom closet and hit the shower.

So much time had passed since he'd been gone from the FBI. Jim had been a good friend and Zach hadn't even acknowledged his wedding. The invitation had likely been tossed with all the mail he'd ignored for so long.

About time he rejoined the human race and pulled his head out of the dark fog he'd sunk into.

JACIE HURRIED TO the main lodge and entered through the back door. Richard had only left them a few moments before; surely he hadn't gone straight to bed. Not with members of his guest list dead and Jacie's sister missing.

As she'd expected, she found him in the resort's office, surrounded by rich wood paneling and bookshelves filling two walls from floor to ceiling.

Richard sat behind his desk, scrubbing a hand over his face.

Jacie cleared her throat.

Her boss glanced up, his eyes bloodshot, the lines beside his eyes and denting his forehead deeper than she'd remembered. "Come in, Jacie." He rose from his chair and rounded his desk, opening his arms to her.

She fell into them, pressing her face against his broad chest. This man had been like a father to her since she'd come to work full-time for him. "Will we get her back?"

"Damn right we will," he said, his voice gruff, his arms tightening around her for a moment. He then pushed her to arm's length. "I've been thinking. Tomorrow at sunup, we'll take the chopper up and do our own search for her. To hell with waiting for the government to get out there. I figure the more people looking, the better."

Jacie stared up at her boss, blinking the tears from her eyes. Richard wasn't good around emotional women, and Jacie made certain she didn't put him in a position to deal with female emotions. She forced a smile, though her lips quivered. "Thank God. I was just coming to ask you if we could use the helicopter."

"I'll do everything in my power to find your sister, Jacie. This should never have happened. I should have done a better background search on those DEA agents."

"You can't blame yourself."

His hands squeezed her arms. "That could be you out there."

She hadn't thought of it that way, and she couldn't now. "But it wasn't."

"Still. I might have lost my best PR woman and trail guide. Do you know how hard it is to find someone like you?" He dropped his hands from her arms and stepped back, running his fingers through his graying hair. "We'll find her. Mark my words." His voice was thick and he appeared to be on the edge of a rare emotional display.

"Thanks." Jacie touched her boss's shoulder. "You and I better get some sleep. We have a long day ahead of us."

He nodded without speaking.

Her chest tight, emotions running high, Jacie left the lodge and returned to her cabin with her first glimmer of hope.

Once inside, with the door closed behind her, she felt the walls press in around her. She paced the inside of her tiny cabin, her heart alternating between settled and crazed. Her sister was out there with terrorists and she could do nothing about it until daylight. The canyons were dangerous enough without the cloak of darkness hiding the animals and drop-offs. It would be suicide to ride back out there. Yet every fiber of her being urged her to do just that.

A woman of action, she felt the inaction eating at her like cancer. Jacie entered the little bedroom, determined to shower and try to rest. Tomorrow would be a long day spent in the canyon. Hopefully they'd find something that would lead them to Tracie.

And to think Tracie had come here to get away from the stress of her job. Some stress relief. Or had she come for an entirely different reason?

Jacie glanced at the phone on the nightstand. Hank had promised to contact the FBI and DEA, but what about Tracie's boyfriend, Bruce Masterson? Granted, he was an FBI agent himself, but large federal agencies like the FBI didn't always communicate to all persons involved.

She hesitated.

Her sister hadn't admitted to any trouble between the two of them, but she hadn't been as excited as she'd been about Bruce the last time Jacie spoke with her on the phone. Still, the man had been Tracie's boyfriend for the past year and had moved in with her six weeks ago. He deserved to know his girlfriend was missing.

Jacie pushed aside her misgivings and reached for the phone, dialing the number Tracie had given when she'd moved in with Bruce.

On the fourth ring, a male, groggy voice answered, "Masterson."

"Bruce?" Jacie asked.

"Tracie?" The grogginess disappeared. "Where are you?"

Bruce's response told Jacie a lot. Tracie hadn't

informed him of her destination. "No, Bruce, this isn't Tracie. It's Jacie, her twin."

"Oh." He paused. "Is Tracie with you?"

"No."

"She's not here, if that's what you wanted to know."

"I know." Jacie dragged in a deep breath. "That's why I'm calling."

"What's wrong?" Bruce demanded. "Is it Tracie? Is she okay?"

A sob rose in her throat and threatened to cut off Jacie's air. "I don't know," she managed, her voice shaking.

"What happened, damn it?" Bruce's voice rose.

"She came to visit the night before last and insisted on coming with me on a hunt." Jacie told Bruce what had happened, her voice ragged, emotion choking her vocal cords. "She's gone, Bruce. Captured by what appears to be members of a Mexican cartel."

For a long moment, Bruce didn't say anything. When he finally spoke, his voice was deadly calm. "I'm coming out there."

"I'm not sure who will be involved. The local law enforcement plans on a search party as soon as it's daylight. We notified the DEA and the FBI and—"

"You notified the FBI already?" Bruce asked. "Why the hell didn't I get word?"

Jacie shrugged, then remembered Bruce couldn't see her. "I don't know. Maybe they're still trying to organize a recovery team. All I know is that my sister is missing and I want her back. Alive."

"Don't worry. I'll be there by morning." The phone clicked in Jacie's ear.

She set it back on the charger, and let out a long steadying breath. The more people she had looking for her sister, the better.

If Jacie planned to be one of the search team, she had to be at her best. A shower and sleep would help her maintain her strength through what looked like a long day ahead.

After thoroughly scrubbing her hair and body, she toweled dry, slipped into a tank top and soft jersey shorts she liked to sleep in and blew her hair dry.

All her movements were rote behavior, her mind on her sister, not the tasks at hand. By the time she stepped out of the small bathroom and into the bedroom, she knew she wouldn't sleep. Her imagination had taken hold and spun all kinds of horrible scenarios Tracie could be enduring. She'd gone over and over all the events of the day, hoping to find one grain of information that might help her locate her sister. And nothing.

The walls closed in around her, and her heart beat hard in her chest, forcing her toward the door and outside, where she felt closer to her sister than anywhere else. She didn't have any other family. Her father and mother had died in a car wreck five years ago, shortly after Jacie finished college. She had no one to turn to, to hold her and tell her it would be all right.

Jacie stared up at the stars, their shine blurred by the rush of tears. Overcome by the events, she sank down on the porch steps and buried her face in her hands, letting the tears flow.

A COOL SHOWER went a long way to waking Zach and clearing his mind, as well as dousing the craving for a strong drink to dull his wits. He lay on the bed, settling on top of a quaint, old-fashioned quilt, not ready to sleep, but hoping he'd find comfort in the reclining position.

The air conditioner struggled to reduce the heat inside the cabin after being off during the hottest part of the day. After fifteen minutes of trying, Zach gave up and rose from the bed. He checked his phone, knowing it hadn't rung and probably wouldn't until the following day.

He wished it was morning already so that he could get started on the search for Jacie's sister. Inaction drove him nuts.

Zach stepped out on the front porch in nothing but his jeans.

The cabin beside his had a soft light glowing

through the window. But it wasn't the window that drew his attention.

A shadowy figure hunkered low on the steps leading up to the porch. Soft sobs reached him across the still of the night.

Careless of his bare feet, Zach left his porch and crossed the short distance to the cabin where Jacie lived.

She didn't hear his approach and Zach took a moment to study her.

Jacie's long, deep-brown hair lay loose about her shoulders, free from the band that had secured it in a ponytail for the hunt. Starlight caught the dark strands, giving her a heavenly blue halo.

Unable to stand still any longer, he climbed the steps.

Her head jerked up and she gasped, her eyes wide, the irises reflecting the quarter moon. "Oh, it's you." She sat up straighter, her hands swiping at the tears. "Shouldn't you be getting some rest?"

"I wanted to know if your boss agreed to using his helicopter."

Jacie sniffed and glanced away. "I didn't have to ask. He volunteered its use. We will leave at sunup." She glanced back at him as she rose. "If that's all, I'll be calling it a night."

Zach should have let her go, but he couldn't, knowing she'd go on to her bed and probably continue her tears into the early morning hours. He reached out and grabbed her arm before she made it to the door. "Your sister is tough. If she's still alive, we'll find her."

Jacie whirled. "Not *if.* My sister is alive. I know it. Either you believe it, or leave." Her chin tipped up and she glared through tear-filled eyes.

A smile tugged at the corners of his mouth. "You two are twins in more ways than one. I wouldn't be going after her if I didn't believe there was a chance of bringing her back alive." He brushed his thumb across her cheek, scraping away an errant tear.

"She has to be." Jacie's lips trembled. "I've gone over and over everything I saw and heard since Tracie got here. There has to be something. Some indication as to what happened. I feel like she came here for a reason."

Zach gripped her arms. "What do you mean?"

"She's never shown up unannounced until last night. Tracie has been all about the bureau since she trained at Quantico. I thought she really missed me, but the more I think about it, the more I realize she wouldn't have come without telling me ahead of time."

"Did she say anything about anyone? Was she working undercover?"

"I asked her why she'd come. She only said to get a break from work and stress." Jacie's eyes narrowed. "What worries me is that when I called her boyfriend, the man she lives with, he didn't know where she'd gone." She glanced up at Zach. "She didn't even tell him where she'd gone."

Zach didn't like it. Something wasn't right about what Jacie was telling him. "Did she say anything about the men you were guiding? Did she give you any indication that she knew them?"

"No and no." Jacie dragged in a deep breath and stared up at the sky. "I wish I'd been more persistent. But she wasn't being very forthcoming with her answers. I didn't want to butt in if she wasn't ready to talk." A single tear slipped free and trailed across her skin. She swiped at it, a frown marring her brow. "Damn it, I never cry."

"It's not a crime." Zach pulled her into his arms and held her, stroking his hand across her hair, the silken strands sifting through his fingers, the scent of honeysuckle wafting around him. She fit perfectly against him, molding to his body, her soft curves belying the strength it took to lead a hunting party into the dry, dusty terrain of Big Bend country.

She wasn't wearing a bra and her breasts pressed into his chest, the material of her shirt providing little barrier between her naked skin and his.

His gut tightened, and without realizing it, his hands slid lower, pulling her hips against his.

After a while, she looked up, her lips full and

far too luscious for a tough hunting guide, her blue-gray eyes limpid pools of ink tinged with the reflection of the stars.

Zach fought the urge to bend closer and capture her lush mouth, his hands tightening around her waist.

Finally he gave in and cupped her cheek. "I'm going to hell for this...but I can't resist." He claimed her lips—gently at first.

When her hands slipped around his neck and drew him closer, he accepted her invitation and crushed her mouth, his tongue pushing past her teeth to slide the length of hers. He wove his fingers through her hair and down her back. Capturing the soft curve of her buttocks, he held her hard against his growing erection.

Her mouth moved over his like a woman starved and hungry for more.

When breathing became necessary, he dragged his lips away and sucked in a deep lungful of air. He dropped her arms and stepped back. "I don't know what the hell just happened, but that was totally unprofessional on my part."

Jacie raised a finger and pressed it to his lips. "Don't. It takes two." She backed a few steps, inching toward the cabin's front door. "I'd better get to bed. Morning will come soon and I want to be awake and alert." She touched a hand to her swollen lips. "Thanks for being here."

Zach pushed his hand through his hair. "Right, I'd better go." He turned, paused and faced Jacie again. "You gonna be all right?"

"Do I have a choice?" Jacie squared her shoulders. "Good night." Then she entered the cabin and closed the door behind her with a soft click.

For a long moment, Zach stood on the porch, his lips tingling from the unexpected kiss and the desire urging him to repeat it.

What the hell had he gotten himself into?

Chapter Five

The alarm clock blasted through the nightmare Jacie had been having, saving her from falling over a cliff in the canyon. She sat straight up and blinked. No sunlight shone through the windows, and a glance at the clock proved it was early.

After lying awake for hours, she must have fallen asleep…for what it was worth. Her dreams had been horrifying, leaving her drained and fatigued more than ever. Used to getting up and going before dawn, she hauled herself out of bed and, in less than five minutes, pulled her hair back into a ponytail, washed her face and ran a toothbrush over her teeth.

Pausing for a brief moment, she stared at her reflection, wondering why a guy as gorgeous as Zach would kiss a woman who didn't wear makeup or fix her hair. She touched a finger to her lips, the memory of Zach's kiss sending shivers across her skin.

"Get a grip," she muttered, and dressed quickly

in jeans, a T-shirt and her well-worn cowboy boots. Ready for the day, she grabbed her cowboy hat and stepped outside onto the porch. The eastern horizon showed signs of the predawn gray inching up the sky. It wouldn't be long before the sun rose and they could take the helicopter over Wild Horse Canyon and hopefully find her sister.

"Sleep much?" A deep, warm voice spoke to her from the corner of her porch.

Jacie gasped and stepped backward, her face heating as the object of her musings chuckled nearby.

Zach's amusement had the opposite effect of setting her heartbeat back to normal.

After their kiss, just being around him took her breath away and made her pulse hammer through her body. What was wrong with her? She hadn't been this aware of a man…ever.

"Did you spend the night on my porch?" she asked, her voice a bit more snappy than she'd have preferred, but then he'd startled and…unnerved her.

He leaned against a thick cedar beam, his arms crossed over his chest, his boots crossed at the ankle, cowboy hat tipped down over his forehead, shadowing his eyes. He appeared relaxed, yet poised to move in a flash. "No. I slept." He tipped his hat back and studied her. "You don't look like you slept at all."

"I take that to mean I look like hell. Gee, thanks." She stepped down one step and stared out at the road leading into the ranch compound. A plume of dust rose in the distance, moving closer at a fast rate. Jacie stepped down one step. "Wonder if that's the FBI or DEA. I thought they'd be basing out of Hank's ranch headquarters since it's closer to the canyon than here."

Zach faced the oncoming vehicle. "I spoke to Hank a few minutes ago. He said both agencies called and are on their way from El Paso but not expected until around noon."

As the vehicle neared, Jacie noted it was a dark pewter pickup with no noticeable markings, and it was coming fast. She dropped down the last two steps and made her way toward the lodge.

Zach followed, his boots crunching in the gravel.

As Jacie rounded the side of the lodge to the front, she noted Richard, Trey, the helicopter pilot, and Richard's other full-time guide, Humberto, standing on the front porch. She and Zach joined them as the truck skidded to a halt in the gravel.

"Expecting someone?" Richard asked.

"No." Jacie's eyes narrowed as a tall man with short-cropped brown hair dropped down from the driver's seat. "Wait, that might be Tracie's boyfriend, Bruce Masterson. He said he'd get here as soon as possible." She glanced at her watch. "He must have broken every speed record between here and San Antonio to make it so quickly. It's okay, he's another FBI agent. Can't hurt having more help finding her."

Zach stood beside Jacie, his bearing stiff, his face unreadable.

The man approached Jacie, frowning. "Jacie?"

"Yes, I'm Jacie." She held out her hand. "And you are?"

"You look so much like your sister, it's uncanny." He climbed the steps and took her hand, staring down into her face. "Bruce Masterson. Tracie's fiancé."

Jacie's eyes widened. "Fiancé? She failed to mention that part. I thought you two were just living together to save on rent."

He gave her a lopsided grin. "Her words. I asked her to marry me before she moved in. She wanted to wait on the engagement, claiming she wasn't ready to settle down. Something about proving herself in the bureau." The smile faded. "Heard anything yet?"

Jacie shook her head. "Nothing."

As if finally aware he and Jacie weren't alone, Bruce glanced at the men gathered. "I assume you're the posse."

Jacie introduced Richard, Humberto and Trey, leaving Zach for last. "And this is my…boyfriend, Zach Adams." For now, it was easier for Bruce to assume Zach was her boyfriend versus her bodyguard. She didn't want any of the focus to shift to herself when her sister was the one who needed to be found.

Bruce tipped his head. "I don't recall Tracie mentioning that you have a boyfriend."

Her skin heated at Bruce's intense stare. "Apparently Tracie needs to work on her communication skills."

Zach shook Bruce's hand. "Don't worry, it's almost as new to you as it is to us. I just showed up recently in the hope of rekindling our college romance." Zach hooked an arm around Jacie's body, pulling her against him. "Seems the feelings are mutual." He pressed a kiss to the top of her head.

Tracie's fiancé's eyes narrowed. "Zach Adams. The name sounds familiar."

Jacie's heart clambered against her ribs. The FBI community was big, but agents ran into each other often. Would Bruce recognize Zach? Did it matter if he knew? Zach hadn't mentioned it to Bruce, so Jacie kept her mouth shut.

"My name's pretty common." Zach's arm dropped from around Jacie. "Our main concern right now is getting Tracie back, safe and sound."

"Right." Richard clapped his hands together. "The chopper has seating for four."

"Chopper?" Bruce's glance shifted to Richard. "The FBI requisitioned a helicopter for the search already?"

"I don't know about that, but we're not waiting." Richard nodded toward Trey. "We have a helicopter we use for scouting out game. Trey is our pilot."

"I'd like to get on board if possible." Bruce glanced from Jacie to Richard.

Jacie shook her head. "Sorry. I'm going."

"Which leaves one seat," Bruce pointed out.

"No, it doesn't." Zach claimed Jacie again by draping an arm over her shoulder. "I go where she goes."

Bruce frowned. "Wouldn't you rather a trained operative help in the search?"

"I've explored canyons before," Zach said. "I know my way around."

"With a weapon?" Bruce argued.

Zach's jaw tightened. "I know how to shoot."

Richard turned to Humberto. "Humberto, you'll take the truck and trailer loaded with two four-wheelers over to Hank's and take off from there." He faced Bruce. "If you're set on going, you can ride with Humberto." Richard pointed his finger at Trey, Zach and Jacie. "You three ready?"

Jacie nodded. "The sooner the better." She pushed aside the horror she'd envisioned of what Tracie was enduring and focused on finding her. "Let's go."

Zach cupped her elbow and led her to the back of the house to the landing pad beside the barn.

"Do you recognize Bruce from your days at the FBI?" Jacie whispered.

"No. But that doesn't mean he didn't recognize me."

"Will it be a problem if he does?"

"We don't know until he comes forward."

Jacie nodded. "In the meantime, you're just my boyfriend from college. By the way, I went to Texas A and M."

He grinned. "Good to know. Have to have our stories straight in case someone asks."

"By the way, where did *you* go to school?"

His mouth twisted into a mischievous hint of a smile. "Now, that would blow my cover if I told you, wouldn't it?"

Richard turned toward Jacie. "I'll take the front with Trey. You two can look out the side windows. We'll head for the ridge overlooking Wild Horse Canyon and go from there."

Jacie nodded. Any effort toward finding her sister was a step in the right direction. She had to focus on that and not on the evasive answer Zach had given her.

She didn't know much about him, other than that he was former FBI and now worked as a cowboy for hire with Hank.

Jacie bit her lip to keep from pressing for more answers and climbed into the helicopter.

Trey handed her a headset and one to Zach.

They tested the communication devices as Trey started the helicopter engine, the noise of the rotors drowning out any attempts at conversation without the headset.

With her seat restraints fastened securely around her, Jacie curled her fingers around the straps and closed her eyes. As she sent up a silent prayer for a safe takeoff and landing and finding her sister, a hand nudged hers.

She opened her eyes.

Zach pulled her fingers free of the belt and wrapped it in his big, warm hand. He didn't say a word but squeezed gently as the helicopter left the ground.

The man didn't even flinch or exhibit any measure of anxiety, as if he'd been up in helicopters on many occasions. Which Jacie wouldn't know, given that he hadn't shared much of his background with her. He was a stranger, yet their kiss made her feel closer to him than the other two men in the helicopter. Jacie had worked with Richard and Trey over the years; Richard was more of a father figure and Trey, an acquaintance with a wife and family waiting for his return in the little town of Wild Oak Canyon.

The helicopter skimmed past the barn and house, rising into a bright blue sky with big fluffy clouds dotting the heavens. It was like any other day, except two men were dead and Jacie's twin was missing.

She concentrated on the ground below, practicing her ability to recognize features before they reached the canyon when it would count.

The truck with the trailer loaded with two four-wheelers flew down the highway below toward the Raging Bull Ranch, making good time.

As they passed to the southeast of Hank Derringer's spread, Jacie made out a gathering of vehicles in the barnyard. True to his word, Hank was on it, organizing locals into a search party. The FBI and DEA would arrive soon and add to the number.

God, she hoped they found Tracie and that she was alive.

ZACH HELD JACIE'S hand throughout the flight.

In less than fifteen minutes, he could make out the ragged edges of a canyon, spreading out below him.

"That's Wild Horse Canyon ahead," Richard's voice crackled over the headset. "Where exactly did you enter the canyon?"

"Farther to the east." Jacie's hand tightened around Zach's fingers as she leaned toward the window, staring at the ground. "There. Right below us. A trail leads down the side of that slope into the canyon. You can see the four-wheeler at the bottom, flipped upside down. The attackers came in from the southwest."

Trey eased the controls to the right and down. The helicopter dipped to the side, swinging toward the narrower fissures in the canyon walls.

"There are so many places to look," Jacie said, her voice staticky in Zach's ear. He recognized the tone of despair the vastness of the canyon must be infusing in her.

"Just look out your window. I'll look out mine. With four people in the air and more following on the ground, we'll cover a lot of territory."

Her fingers squeezed his and she shot him a grateful look.

Zach would rather continue to stare at the fresh-faced woman than at the ground, but he pulled his attention back to the task at hand. Getting involved with the client went against his training as an agent. He knew the risks. He'd learned his lesson when he'd fallen in love with Toni. Don't get involved. It led to heartache. In his line of work, he was better off remaining aloof, impartial and alone.

He glanced at the hand he held and almost let go.

At that exact moment, Jacie's fingers tightened. "What's that?"

"Where?"

"Down there," she said, her voice tight, strained.

"In that J-shaped curve. I thought I saw a reflection of light off something metal." Her gaze didn't waver as Trey circled around and brought the chopper closer.

Zach peered out his side of the aircraft as the chopper banked back to the left. "I see it. We won't get any closer in this. We'll have to find a clearing to land."

Trey rose again, his head turning back and forth. "I can't land here. I'll have to take it back the way we came a bit."

Jacie rocked in her seat. "It might be her. Oh, dear Lord, let it be Tracie."

In the middle of making a wide circle, a loud bang caused the helicopter to lurch to the side.

"Holy crap! Our rudder's been hit." Trey's urgent announcement riffled through Zach's headset. "I'm losing directional control. I have to land now, before I lose it all. Brace yourself."

As the chopper started a slow spin, Jacie stared at Trey struggling with the controls. Then she looked at Zach.

He turned toward her and cupped her face. "Hold on. I gotcha." He let his fingers slide down her arm and he clutched her hand again, bending forward, and urging her to do the same.

The helicopter rotors turned, easing the aircraft down between the tight walls of the canyon.

If they tipped even slightly to either side, the

blades would hit the rocks and that would be the end of their search and possibly the end of their lives.

Zach wanted to pull Jacie into his arms and protect her from the rough landing, but they were better off trusting the seat belts. He'd save the embrace for when they landed safely.

The ground seemed to spin up to meet them faster than Zach liked. At the last moment before the skids hit the uneven surface, he prayed the first prayer he'd made since Toni's death.

The chopper hit the ground, jolting Zach so hard his teeth rattled. The scent of aviation fuel filled the air. He waited several seconds for any shifting before he flung off his belt and reached for Jacie's.

"I can't get it to unbuckle." Her hands shook as she fought with the release clamp.

Zach brushed aside her fingers and flicked it open, then dragged her across the seat and out into the open, away from the damaged craft.

Trey shut down the engine and scrambled out of the pilot's seat. Richard joined him beside Zach and Jacie.

Everyone tugged their headsets off and stared at the downed helicopter.

"What happened?" Richard asked.

"I'd get closer to investigate, but with fuel leaking, it's best to stay back until we're sure it won't create a fire." Trey sucked in a deep breath and let it out, visibly shaken by the experience. "I've never had that happen here."

"Why did the helicopter shake so hard before it lost the rudder?" Jacie asked.

"We were hit by something, hard in the tail."

"What? A bird?"

"No, more like a rocket."

"Who in the hell has rockets out here?" Richard demanded.

Zach's body grew rigid. "Maybe we shouldn't stand so close to the helicopter and seek some cover. The cartels have this kind of ammunition. Either provided illegally by the black market or stolen from the Mexican Army. Whatever, we're in hostile territory and should treat it as such." He grabbed Jacie's hand and dragged her toward an outcropping.

The woman dug her heels into the rocky soil. "No. We can't give up the search now. What about the metal reflection? It could be a vehicle. They could be holding Tracie nearby." She jerked her hand free and headed back the way they'd come in the chopper. "We have to check it out."

Zach sighed. She was right. Though he didn't like the idea of being trapped in a canyon with the possibility of being shot at, he had to either catch up with Jacie or risk her being taken as easily as her sister, or killed like the DEA Agents.

"Will you at least wait over there in the shadows until I get some more firepower?"

She frowned. "You can't go back to the chopper. It might explode."

He smiled. "I'd rather risk an explosion than walk off into a desert canyon underarmed."

She bit her bottom lip for a moment. "Okay, but hurry."

Zach nodded to Richard. "Get her over there, will ya?"

The Big Elk Ranch owner's brows furrowed. "Let me get the guns. No use you losing it on my chopper."

"Please, just make sure she's under cover."

"I'm coming with you," Trey insisted.

Zach rushed back to the chopper, grabbed four weapons hooked over the backs of the seat. He tossed two rifles to Trey and checked the other two. Each was fully loaded, safeties on. With the weapons slung over his shoulder, he and Trey ran back to where Richard and Jacie stood in the shadows of the overhanging cliffs.

Zach handed Jacie a rifle. "Know how to use one?"

She snorted. "You have to ask?"

"She's a better shot than I am," Richard admitted, taking the rifle Trey handed him. "Let's go."

On the alert for any movement, high or low, Zach took point. If they'd been shot down by a rocket, no telling what other armament the cartel had in their arsenal. He didn't like being at the bottom of the canyon, basically sitting ducks for anyone standing guard on the rim. They didn't have much choice if they wanted to get to the point where Jacie had spotted the metal reflection.

"Up ahead," Jacie called out in a husky whisper. "That's the lower end of the J-shaped crevice. What I spotted was just on the other side of that curve." She hurried to catch up with Zach.

His arm shot out and clotheslined her at the chest. He pressed a finger to his lips and waited until she made eye contact with him. "I'll take lead. No use all of us charging in and getting shot. Let me scout ahead and see what's up there. I'll whistle if all's clear."

"But—"

Zach held up his hand. "One person can move silently. Four have less of a chance."

Richard's hands descended on Jacie's shoulders. "He's right. In fact, maybe we should wait and let the FBI or DEA go in. They are better trained and equipped to handle a situation like this."

"I can do this," Zach reassured him.

Jacie nodded. "Let him. He knows what he's doing. I'll stay until you whistle."

Zach took off, the rifle slung over his shoulder, his handgun in his right hand, safety off, ready for whatever lay ahead.

He eased through the shadows, careful not to disturb the loose rocks and gravel as he rounded the corner of the rocky escarpment. On the ground beside him, he noted tire tracks. Whoever had come this way had come on what looked like an ATV. One larger than the four-wheeler back at the canyon rim.

Zach stopped several times to listen. Not a single noise reached him or echoed off the walls of the canyon. He moved forward and finally rounded the curve leading back the other way. An all-terrain vehicle with seating for four stood smashed against a rock. Two bodies lay motionless, one slumped over the steering wheel, the other crumpled down in the passenger seat.

Without making a sound. Zach stood so still he could have blended in with the rocks themselves, his gaze panning the immediate vicinity and the rocky ledges above. Nothing moved; nothing made a sound. Several vultures circled high above.

Zach stepped out into the open, crouched low, ready to duck and run if shots rang out. He eased over to the vehicle and checked for a pulse. Both men were dead, their bodies stiff, skin purple and eyes sunken. Rigor mortis had set in. These men had been dead for at least four hours.

Zach climbed halfway up a slope and stared around. As far as he could tell, he was alone.

As he puckered to whistle, a movement caught his eye at the base near the corner he'd just come around.

He reached for the rifle and stopped when he realized it was Jacie, doing as he'd done, easing around the base of the canyon walls, sticking to the shadows.

Zach's jaw tightened and he slipped quietly down the slope coming up behind Jacie as she worked her way toward the vehicle, her attention on the bodies within, not the world around her.

Zach waited between two rocks until she came within range.

"Bang. You're dead," he said.

Chapter Six

Jacie gasped and swung her rifle around.

Before she could point it and pull the trigger, the man hiding in the crevice knocked the weapon from her hands, spun her back around, twisting her arm up between her shoulder blades. He cinched his arm around her neck, limiting her air.

"Let me go." She bucked against his hold, her body stiff, her feet kicking outward to throw him off balance. "Or I'll—"

He held her steady, as if she were nothing but a child. "Or you'll what?" he whispered against her ear. "You're in no position to threaten or bargain."

"Zach?" She froze, all the fight left her and she sagged against him. "Damn it, Zach, you scared the crap out of me."

He turned her in his arms, refusing to release her yet. And frankly Jacie was glad. She hadn't liked it when he'd walked away and stayed gone for so long she thought he'd fallen over a cliff or had been captured. His strong arms around her brought back that feeling of safety at the same time it spelled danger of a completely different kind.

"I could have been one of the drug runners." He brushed his thumb over her cheek, pushing a strand of her hair that had escaped her ponytail behind her ear. "You could have been shot and killed or worse—taken in by the same terrorists who have your sister."

Her breath hitched in her throat, and her blood rushed through her veins like the Rio Grande in flood stages. His body pressed to hers, warm, sexy and overwhelming. "You've made your point. I should have stayed put."

"Yes, you should have."

"I couldn't stand waiting, not knowing whether you were all right, or if you'd found Tracie." She stared up into his eyes.

He kissed her, a brief brush of his lips, and set her at arm's length. "She's not here."

JACIE'S LIPS TINGLED and she fought back the urge to cry. Instead she squared her shoulders. "So, what's all this?" She waved her hand toward the abandoned vehicle and the dead men. "What can we learn from what we found? There has to be a clue as to who took her." She moved toward the four-by-four, bracing herself for what she'd see. The two dead men last night had been partially cloaked in darkness and still looked fairly normal. These two had been dead longer and were a waxy zombielike purple. "How long do you suppose they've been here?" Her gag reflex threatened to choke her.

"At least four hours. Maybe longer."

"Not long after they took Tracie," Jacie noted. A shiver shook her from head to toe. She had to remind herself that Tracie might not be here, but at least she wasn't one of the bodies left behind.

"Holy hell, Jacie, don't ever do that again." Richard burst into the open, huffing and puffing, followed by Trey. Behind them Humberto and Bruce emerged.

"We brought reinforcements," Trey offered.

Bruce stepped forward and studied the two bodies without touching them. "Looks like members of La Familia Diablos."

Zach stiffened, his face going pale beneath his tan.

Had Jacie not looked at him at that exact moment, she'd have missed his reaction to Bruce's words.

"How do you know?" Jacie asked.

Bruce pointed to the tattoo on the driver's right shoulder, the tail of a dragon dipping below his T-shirt sleeve. "The Diablos all have a dragon tattoo on their right arms. If you push the other man's sleeve up, you'll likely find one similar to this one."

"I'll take your word for it." Jacie had no intention of touching either of the two dead men. Instead she inched toward Zach, taking comfort in his presence. "Why would they kill their own people?"

"Who said they did?" Bruce glanced across the dead man at Jacie. "There are two crime families in this area—Los Lobos and La Familia Diablos. Any chance they get to kill each other off, they'll take it. My bet is the Diablos took Tracie and the Los Lobos ambushed them. Since Tracie isn't here among the dead, thank God, they must have her in the Los Lobos camp."

Humberto stood to the side, his eyes narrowed, his face grim. "The Diablos will avenge their *compadres'* deaths."

"Will they attack Los Lobos?" Jacie's hand reached for Zach's.

"Probably," Bruce responded. "It'll be a bloodbath."

Her fingers tightened around Zach's. "Then we have to get to Tracie before the Diablos do."

"It's not that easy," Zach said quietly. "I've heard they have tightly guarded compounds on the other side of the border. No one gets in or out without running a gauntlet of killer guards."

"But we can't give up now." Jacie stared toward

the south as if she could see the camp from where they stood in the canyon. "Tracie's still alive. I just know it. But for how long…" She turned back to Zach.

His face was set in grim lines and his lips remained tightly shut.

"There's nothing you can do but let the FBI and DEA handle this." Bruce touched Jacie's shoulder. "I'll get with them and explain my assessment. They'll decide whether or not to launch an attack and when. But as far as you and the members of the Big Elk Ranch are concerned, you should step back and let the pros handle it from here."

Zach's fingers tightened painfully around Jacie's.

"But—" Jacie couldn't let it go. She just couldn't stand back and do nothing.

"Jacie." Zach tugged her hand and forced her to face him. "He's right."

Bruce took charge. "You guys can double up on the four-wheelers to get back to the truck. Humberto and I can stay until two of you can come back to get us."

Zach raised a hand. "Jacie and I will stay back."

"I'd rather get her out of the canyon. If there was even a chance either of the gangs is still here, she'd be in danger. It's bad enough one of the Kosart women is already a captive." Bruce turned to Humberto. "You're okay with staying, aren't you?"

"No," Richard said. "The men killed last night and Tracie were my responsibility. I should be the one to stay with Mr. Masterson. Besides, Humberto needs to lead the way out of the canyon."

"I'd rather keep Humberto. No offense, Mr. Giddings. He's probably faster on his feet."

Richard's eyes narrowed. "You might be right about that. I'm not getting any younger." He turned to Zach and Jacie. "Come on, the sooner we get the two of you out of here, the sooner I can get back down here and retrieve these two gentlemen."

Jacie wanted to argue, but she didn't know what else they could do without horses or additional four-wheelers to track the men responsible for kidnapping Tracie. She climbed on one of the ATVs and pressed the start button.

Zach slung his leg over the back and sat behind her, his arms circling her waist, holding on tight.

Without a word, she twisted the throttle and the cycle shot forward.

Zach's arms tightened, his hard, muscled chest pressing against Jacie's back. It wasn't long before they climbed the narrow trail out of the canyon and came to a stop beside the truck and trailer.

Jacie waited for Zach to dismount before she got off.

Richard and Trey topped the rise and pulled up beside them. Trey climbed off.

"I'm going back for Humberto," Richard said.

"I'm going with you." Jacie turned the four-wheeler in a tight circle.

When she came to a halt, Zach grabbed her handlebar. "Let Trey." His stare was intense.

She'd hoped to check out the murder scene one last time before she gave up and called their search a failure. "No, I want to go."

"Jacie." Richard pulled up beside her. "Trey can handle this. You stay here." It wasn't a request. Her boss meant business.

She got off the bike.

Trey mounted and the two men rode back down into the canyon.

As they disappeared over the ridgeline, Jacie's vision blurred, and she fought back tears of anger and frustration. "I thought you were supposed to help me."

"I am." Zach gripped her arms and turned her to face him. "There's more to this than either of us can handle on our own."

"But she's my sister!" Jacie pounded her fists against his chest. "I can't just stand by and do nothing."

"We won't. We can do some work behind the scenes. There has to be people on the ranch or in the town who know what's going on and can help us find your sister."

"You think we can learn anything back there?" Jacie waved at the canyon. "Tracie disappeared there."

"But she knew enough to follow those men into the canyon. She knew something, and we need to find out what it was. It might be the key to who took her and where they might be holding her." Zach pulled her into his arms. "Hank hired me because he had faith in my abilities as an agent. He trusted me to do the job." Zach tipped her chin up and stared into her eyes. "I need you to trust me too."

This man hadn't shown her much of anything yet. How could she trust him? She knew nothing about him. For a long moment Jacie stared up into Zach's dark gaze. Something about the way he held her and the sorrow buried deep in his liquid brown eyes made her say, "I trust you."

For several long seconds, he held her, his gaze unwavering. Then he bent his head and kissed her.

Jacie should have pushed him away, but that rational idea didn't even enter her head. Instead she wrapped her arms around his neck and dragged him closer, needing the comfort of his arms, the pressure of his mouth on hers, if only to chase away the fear of losing her only sister.

But it was more than that. This man had known

suffering. His heart still bore the scars, and despite his apparent effort to hide them, he wore them on his sleeve.

All thoughts melted away as the kiss deepened. Jacie's tongue pushed past Zach's teeth and slid along his, thrusting and tasting the hint of coffee and mint.

His fingers dug into her buttocks, smashing her against him, the evidence of her effect on him pressing into her belly.

Jacie didn't know how long they stood, locked in the embrace. The world around them faded away, leaving them alone, until the sound of a hawk crying out overhead dragged her back to the real world.

She forced her hands between them and pushed against his chest. "What are we doing?"

Zach ran a hand through his hair and sighed. "I'm sorry. That shouldn't have happened...."

"Again," she concluded. "Why can't I keep my hands off you?" She stared down at the offending digits. "This effort isn't about you and me. It's about bringing my sister back alive."

"And the sooner we get back to civilization, we can work on that."

A hole the size of Texas opened in Jacie's heart and she looked across at Zach. "We will get her back, won't we?"

"We will." Zach's gaze bore into hers, his dark

brown eyes so intense they appeared black. If anyone would fight to free her sister, Zach would. But he'd do it his way. Not ride off without a plan.

ZACH SAT IN the backseat of the king cab pickup with Jacie beside him. Richard drove, Humberto rode shotgun and Bruce and Trey sat in the truck bed. Since the others had returned, Zach hadn't spoken a word, his mind churning over what he'd learned and the information he still required to determine the whereabouts of Tracie Kosart.

As Bruce had said, the dead men in the four-by-four had been members of the Diablos. As soon as Zach had seen the tattoos, he'd known. He'd studied the gangs prior to taking the assignment to infiltrate the Diablos gang area in the border town of El Paso. He and Toni had crossed into Juarez as honeymooning tourists. Only someone in the bureau must have leaked the fact that they were undercover agents. Within twenty-four hours, they'd been captured and the rest was the awful history he would never forget.

His hands clenched into fists. If Los Lobos knew Tracie was FBI, she'd be in for the same treatment as Toni.

Zach's gut knotted. He vowed to himself to find her before they went too far. He glanced at Jacie. She was better off not knowing what her sister faced. It would only make her more reckless and determined to go to her sister's rescue. One lone woman against an army of thugs.

She sat quietly staring out the window as if she might see her sister walk out across the dry Texas land. Her forehead was creased with worry lines.

As soon as they got back to the ranch, Zach would start asking questions. If there were cartel members crossing the border nearby, there were cartel members on the U.S. side aiding them.

As soon as the truck pulled up to the Big Elk Lodge, Zach jumped down and rounded the truck to assist Jacie. She'd already slipped from her seat and stood beside the truck. "What next?"

Zach cupped her elbow and turned toward the other men. "If you need us, we'll be in town." He gave half a smile. "Seems I left home in such a hurry I forgot a few things I hope to pick up at the local stores."

"We have shaving cream, razors and toothbrushes in the lodge, if that's what you're missing," Richard offered.

"Thanks, but I'd rather go to town." Zach winked at the owner of the Big Elk. "Getting away will help keep Jacie occupied while the FBI and DEA do their thing."

Richard nodded at Jacie. "Don't worry, darlin'. They'll get her back."

Jacie's lips formed a tight smile. "I know." Her entire countenance read *failure is not an op-*

tion. Zach could have kissed her again. She was strong and tough. The few tears she'd shed had been more out of frustration and real fear for her sister's life.

"Come on, honeycakes." He led her away from the group toward the tiny cabin where she lived. "We'll take my truck. It's not as well known around town."

"Where are we going?"

"To Wild Oak Canyon."

She let him open her door as she turned to face him. "Why are we really going to town?"

"Your sister came to visit, and from what it looks and sounds like, she had an idea that something was going to go down last night, or she wouldn't have insisted on riding out with you and the two DEA agents."

"So what does that have to do with going to town?"

"How did she find out about who and what might be happening?"

"Through her contacts at the FBI?"

"It might have started there, but she wasn't the only one around here who knew something was going to happen. Those DEA agents wouldn't have gone down into that canyon without backup if they'd thought they were in danger."

"You think they were expecting to meet someone who wasn't going to be shooting at them?"

"Yes." Zach rounded the truck and climbed up into the driver's seat. "There have to be other people nearby who knew what was going to happen. Cartel members like to brag about their kills and ambushes." He paused with his fingers on the key in the ignition. "If we find the right people, we might discover who knows something, like who's responsible and where they're holding your sister."

Jacie's eyes lit. "Then what are we waiting for? Go!"

Zach twisted the key and set the truck in motion, heading down the long, dusty gravel driveway. "Now, don't get your hopes up. Cartel members tend to be pretty close-lipped around strangers."

Jacie slammed a fist into her palm. "Then we'll beat the information out of them."

Zach chuckled. "That's my girl. Tough as nails and soft as silk."

Her cheeks flamed. "I'm not your girl," she muttered. "And I'm not soft." She stared at her work-roughened fingers. "And 'honeycakes'? Really, was that all you could come up with?"

Zach chuckled, betting she was soft in all the right places, and "honeycakes" was perfect.

He shook himself and forced his attention back to the road, headed into Wild Oak Canyon.

"Where does everyone go at one point or another to talk or share a cup of coffee?"

"That would be Cara Jo's Diner," Jacie said. "She's a friend of mine. Everyone has dinner there at least once a week to catch up on everyone else's business."

"Good. We'll start there."

Chapter Seven

Jacie entered the diner first, her nostrils filling with the comforting smells of meat loaf, roasted chicken and fried okra. Once Zach passed through the door and it closed behind him, Jacie paused, closed her eyes and inhaled deeply, letting the aromas calm her.

"Smells like home."

Jacie opened her eyes and tipped her head toward Zach.

A smile tugged at the corners of his lips.

This was perhaps the first clue he'd given her about his life outside his work. "Did your mother make her kitchen smell that good?"

"Always. She loved to cook and we always had great food." His smile faded. "I miss her."

"What happened?"

"She and my father had me late in life. And all that good cooking clogged their arteries." He sighed. "They died within months of each other. Mom couldn't imagine life without Dad." Something about the grim set of his lips spoke more than his words.

"Where were you during all this?" Jacie asked.

"I wasn't there when Dad had his heart attack."

"Were you working for the FBI then?"

He nodded.

"Undercover?"

Again he nodded. "I didn't know until it was almost too late to see my mother before she passed too."

Jacie's chest tightened. She and Tracie had lost both their parents to an automobile accident. "At least you got to say goodbye to your mother," she said quietly. Then she squared her shoulders. "How about that booth in the corner?"

"I'd prefer to sit at the bar. We might learn more there."

"Right."

As she strode across the floor, Cara Jo, the diner's owner, pushed open the swinging door to the kitchen with her hip and carried a large tray full of steaming entrees to a table of cowboys. "I'll be with you in a minute. Seat yourself," she called out.

Cara Jo's shoulder-length, light brown hair swung as she spun around in her cute little waitress outfit. The retro-styled dress that hadn't fazed Jacie in the least in the past suddenly made her more aware of her dusty jeans and even dirtier shirt. Her face probably had the same layer of grime and her hair… "We'll take a seat at the bar," Jacie said.

"Suit yourself." Cara Jo laid out one full plate at a time in front of the cowboys. No sooner had she set a plate on the colorful gingham tablecloth than a cowboy practically stabbed her with a fork, diving into the vittles.

Jacie chuckled. "Cara Jo has the best food in the county."

"Isn't this the only diner in the county?"

"Only one that's stayed in business. People come back when the food's this good." She stopped at the bar. "I'm going to wash up. I'll be right back."

"Me, too. I can still smell aviation fuel and dead men." Zach wrinkled his nose. "Back in two shakes."

While Zach headed for the men's room, Jacie pushed through the door of the ladies' room.

What she saw in the mirror was worse than she'd imagined. Brown hair stuck out of the loosened ponytail, in complete disarray, windblown, not in a good way, and tinged gray with dust. Her face had a layer of fine Texas sand over it, giving her a sun-dried, tanned look that wasn't any more appealing than it sounded. When she patted her shirt, a cloud rose from her and she coughed.

Holy hell, you'd think she had more pride than

to show up in town looking like…well, like one of the cowboys. People expected the men to look wind worn and filthy. But a woman was supposed to have more pride.

She squared her shoulders and stared into the mirror. "Why do I care? My sister is missing and no one really cares about how I look." Except herself. She yanked the ponytail out of her hair, bent over, her long brown hair hanging down, and ran her fingers through the thick tresses, shaking out the dust. When she flipped it back, it was better. Not great, but better.

She patted her shirt, flapped it to get the dust to fly loose, then slapped at her jeans. The light in the room grew hazy.

"This is crazy. It's not like the man sees me as anything more than the job." She sighed. "Oy, but that kiss…"

Jacie splashed her face with water from the sink, wishing she had a little lip gloss to coat her dry lips. Who was she kidding?

Semisatisfied that she didn't look like a complete loser, she stepped out of the bathroom and ran into a hard wall of muscle.

Zach caught her in his arms and steadied her. "Do you always talk to yourself in the bathroom?"

Her cheeks burned and she grimaced up at him. "Are the walls that thin?"

He nodded.

Mortified, she couldn't bring herself to ask how much he'd overheard. "Well, then, we should start our investigation." She hurried past him, hoping he'd only heard her mumbling.

"Just so you know, you're not just the job," he called out softly behind her.

Jacie was sure her face couldn't get any hotter. She plopped into a bar stool and gave Cara Jo all her attention. "Could I get a glass of ice water?"

"You bet. Guess it's getting pretty hot out there already." Cara Jo snagged a full, frosty pitcher, poured two glasses of ice water and set them in front of Jacie and Zach. "Jacie, sweetie, who's your handsome friend?"

Jacie stiffened at Cara Jo's flirty query. "Zach Adams."

"Her boyfriend from college," Zach interjected.

Cara Jo's eyebrows furrowed, a smile playing at her lips. "You never told me you had a boyfriend from college." Still holding the pitcher of water, she planted her fist on one hip and looked down her nose. "Come on, tell all."

"Not much to tell." Jacie hated lying to her only friend outside the Big Elk Ranch. "We met in college."

"Well, it must have been more than a chance meeting for him to show up here after all these years."

"I missed her." Zach slid an arm around Jacie's

waist, his breath stirring the hairs around her neck, making gooseflesh rise on her arms.

Jacie couldn't continue the lie and she had more important things on her mind. She sucked in a long, steadying breath. "Cara Jo, Tracie's missing."

Cara Jo plunked the pitcher on the counter. "Oh, my God. How? When?" She reached across the counter and gathered Jacie's hands in hers. "Oh, baby, you must be beside yourself. And to think, she was just in here the day before yesterday."

"That's when she got in town." Jacie gave her the bare-bones details of what had occurred since.

"Holy hell, Jacie, you were almost killed." She rounded the counter and hugged her friend. "What about Tracie? Do you have any idea where they might have taken her? Have the FBI and DEA arrived? Have they mounted a search and rescue?"

Jacie gave a wry chuckle. "Slow down, will ya? We have no idea where they took her and yes, the FBI and DEA are on it. But I can't just sit around and wait for them to find her. I have to do something."

"Honey, what *can* you do? You're not trained to fight the Mexican cartel. Hell, even the soldiers and agencies who *are* can't seem to slow them down." Cara Jo stopped talking when she looked Jacie in the face. "Sorry. I'm not helping, am I?" She squeezed Jacie's shoulders and stepped back around the counter. "What can I do? Want me to join the search party? I will."

"No." Jacie shook her head. "They want me to stay out of it. What I need is to find out anything I can about when my sister came to town. Did she talk to anyone? Meet anyone here in the diner? Say anything?"

Cara Jo pinched the bridge of her nose. "She asked for directions to the Big Elk Ranch.... Think, Cara." For a long moment she said nothing. Finally she looked up. "I seem to recall her talking to a man outside the diner."

"Did you see him? Who was it?"

"I don't know. He was dark haired, maybe Hispanic. Not very tall." Cara Jo's eyes widened. "Wait a minute. If I remember correctly, someone was sitting at the window booth staring out at the same time Tracie was talking to the man." Cara Jo's lips twisted into a grimace. "Oh, yeah. It was Bull Sarly. Maybe you can get that cantankerous old man to tell you who it was."

Jacie bit her lip. "All we can do is try. Maybe if he knows how important it is to find her quickly..."

"Yeah." Cara Jo snorted. "Good luck with that." She raised a finger. "If you're planning on going out there, I have something you'll need." She hurried into the kitchen and emerged a minute later with a wad of white butcher paper. "You'll need this."

Jacie smiled. "Thanks."

"Cara Jo, can you remember anything else?" Zach asked. "A conversation, maybe not between Tracie and anyone else, but one that might have to do with a meeting in Wild Horse Canyon?"

Cara Jo shook her head. "Nothing like that. I'll tell you what, though, the whole time your sister was here, she kept fiddling with her cell phone. She'd press a button, put it to her ear and then take it down and end the call before it even had time to ring. I thought it was weird at the time but figured the line was busy or something."

"Cara Jo." A pretty blonde with a miniature version of herself sitting beside her in a booth waved her hand. "Can I get a cup of milk for Lily?"

Jacie's friend smiled at the woman and called out, "Got it." Then she focused on Jacie again. "Hey, would you like to meet Kate and Lily? They just moved into the old Kendrick place."

"Maybe next time I'm in town." Jacie liked meeting people, but her sister took priority over socializing.

"I understand." Cara Jo pulled a carton of milk out of a refrigerator under the counter and poured a plastic cup full, snapped a lid on it and stuck in a straw. "It was good to meet you, Zach. I'd hang around and chat, but I have to work. My waitress called in sick. Let me know if I can do anything to help. I can shut down the diner in a heartbeat and be ready."

"Thanks, Cara Jo. I'd appreciate it if you'd keep your ears open." Jacie reached across the bar and squeezed Cara Jo's hand. "If anything comes up in a conversation that might relate to Tracie's disappearance, call me."

"You bet I will."

While Cara Jo waited on the tables, Jacie swallowed some of the ice water and stood. "Let's go find Bull Sarly."

"I take it you know the man." Zach cupped her elbow and escorted her from the diner as if she were dressed in a fine dress at a cocktail party instead of wearing jeans and a dusty T-shirt.

Jacie hated to admit it, but she liked it. After working at the ranch for the past few years, she'd almost forgotten what it was like to be treated like a lady. She'd made it a point to be one of the guys. The men trusted her as a guide more if she looked like one of them. For a long time, it had seemed like an asset, her ability to blend in with the menfolk. Since she'd met Zach, the ability seemed more a liability.

ZACH PULLED OUT onto Main Street. "Where does Mr. Sarly live?"

Jacie blew out a breath. "On a small plot of

land west of town. Out by the dump." She glanced at Zach. "Let me warn you, he's a cranky old geezer. Never has anything good to say about anyone. We'll be lucky if he tells us anything. Hell, we'll be lucky to get past his rottweiler, Mo."

"We'll manage." Zach had been shot at, beat up and tortured in his line of work. What kind of grief could one cranky old man give him that he hadn't already overcome?

Five miles west of the town of Wild Oak Canyon, Jacie motioned for him to pull off the road onto a rutted track that looked more like a shallow ravine than a road. It wound through clumps of saw palmetto and prickly pear cactus, the vegetation like so much concertina wire strung along a perimeter.

"I take it Mr. Sarly doesn't get many visitors," Zach remarked, bracing himself for a meeting with the man.

"He doesn't want any. He's said as much."

"Sometimes a man might push others away to keep from being hurt. Perhaps Mr. Sarly was hurt by a woman or lost someone he loved and hasn't gotten over it."

"Uh-huh. Or he's just plain cranky and doesn't like people at all. I always give him the benefit of the doubt. But he always gives it right back in my face." Jacie shook her head. "You can't please all of the people."

"True." As they rounded a patch of scrawny mesquite trees, a tired, gray-weathered wooden house came into view. Sitting on the porch with a shotgun in his lap was a big man wearing only a faded pair of blue jeans and old brogan boots. His gut hung over his waistband and his long gray, shaggy hair blended into an equally long and shaggy beard, neither of which had been combed or cut in at least a decade. A husky red-and-black rottweiler lounged on the porch beside the man's chair, seemingly unconcerned by the approach of a strange vehicle.

Zach pulled to a halt out of range of the shotgun's blast.

When Jacie moved to open her door, Zach held out a hand. "I'll handle this."

"But—"

"Please."

Jacie shrugged. "Here, you might want this." She handed him the package wrapped in white butcher paper he'd all but forgotten.

With a frown, Zach held up the package. "What's this for?"

She grinned. "The dog."

As soon as Zach's boots touched the ground, the dog leaped off the deck and raced toward him.

"Throw the package," Jacie yelled.

Without thinking, Zach did as Jacie said and threw the package at the dog.

The rottweiler ground to a halt, sniffed at the offering and then clamped his teeth around it. He then trotted off into the brush.

"Damned good-fer-nothin' hound," Bull Sarly grumbled from the porch.

After the dog left, Zach headed for the porch. "Mr. Sarly."

"Ain't no mister up here."

"Bull Sarly?" Zach continued toward the man with the shotgun.

"That'd be me. Ya got twenty seconds to state yer piece. Take that numbskull that long to rip into whatever you brought for him. And I'll be shootin' whatever's left after the dog's finished with ya."

"Then I'll speak fast." Zach never let his gaze drift from the old man's. He studied the way the gnarled fingers tightened around the worn wooden stalk of the gun in his lap, anticipating any aggressive move on the other man's part.

"Tracie Kosart was kidnapped yesterday by Mexican cartel."

"So? I ain't no Mexican cartel. Get off my property."

"You were at the diner day before yesterday when she came in."

"Man's got a right to eat." He held up a hand. "You can stop right there."

Zach halted at the base of the steps, directly in

front of the old man, his jaw tight, his knees bent slightly, ready to spring. "Before she came into the diner, she spoke with a short Hispanic man. You sat in the booth staring out at them. Can you identify the man?"

"I could..." The old man stuck a straw in his mouth and sneered. "If I gave a rat's behind."

Zach's blood boiled. While this man lorded himself over them, Tracie Kosart could be suffering horrible torture. Frustrations of the past day, no, the past two years exploded in one flying leap.

Zach climbed the steps, grabbed the shotgun, jerked it out of the curmudgeon's hands and flung it across the yard. Then he lifted the man to his feet and slammed him up against the wall of the house. "How about right now?"

The man's eyes bulged, his face and body breaking out in a sweat. "You ain't got no right to push me around on my own property. I'll have your job for this. Let me go," he gasped, scratching at the fingers pressing into his windpipe.

"You're assuming I care about my job." Zach pushed the man higher up the wall until his feet dangled. "I don't. However, I do care about finding a woman who could very well be raped, tortured and killed. Preferably before all three of those things happen." He shook the man. "Now, are you going to tell me something that will help me find her, or do I make you sorry you didn't?"

"Zach. Don't." Jacie's voice called out behind him.

"Listen to the girl," Sarly whined. "Won't do you no good if you knock me out or kill me."

"Please." Jacie's hand touched Zach's arm.

A blast of calm washed over Zach's raging nerves. Still, he wanted to beat someone's head in, and Bull Sarly was just enough of a pain in the butt to deserve it.

The hand on his arm tightened. "He's not worth going to jail over," she whispered.

"And your sister's not worth saving?" Zach rasped.

"Yes, she is, but this isn't going to help."

"Sister?" Bull stared from Zach to Jacie. "You didn't say nothin' 'bout that woman being yer sister. Let me down. Maybe I know somethin'.'"

Zach held him there a second longer, then let go so fast the man slid down the wall before his legs engaged and held up his bulk.

"Talk fast. A woman's life depends on us finding her sooner than later."

Jacie stepped up to the man and touched his arm. "Mr. Sarly, the cartel took my sister. We think she might have spoken to someone the day she came to town who might know where they would have taken her. Please." Her eyes filled with tears. "She's my only living relative. I'd do anything to save her."

A growl sounded behind Zach.

As Sarly had indicated, once the dog had finished the treat, he was back and ready to take up where he'd left off.

Zach pulled the pistol from his shoulder holster and aimed it at the dog. "Call him off or I'll shoot him."

"Don't." Sarly raised a hand. "Like your sister, Mo is the only family I have." He gave the rottweiler a stern look. "Sit."

A long moment passed as the dog growled low in its throat, knowing a threat when he saw it and ready to launch an attack to the death.

Zach's weapon remained trained on the dog.

"Sit, damn you." Sarly pushed to his feet and took a step toward the dog.

Mo squatted on his haunches, his lip still pulled back in a menacing snarl.

"Good boy." The older man patted his leg. "Come."

The dog trotted up the steps to his master and sat at his feet.

Zach let out the breath he'd been holding. He liked dogs and hadn't wanted to shoot the creature. But he would have, if it was Jacie's or his life over the dog's.

"Look, I don't want nothin' to happen to yer

sister, any more than you do." Bull scratched his beard. "I seem to recall her lookin' just like you and I really thought it was you until she asked for directions to the Big Elk." He snorted. "Didn't even know you had a twin."

Jacie gave him the hint of a smile. "Not many people do."

"Did you recognize the man she spoke to outside the diner?" Zach pushed. The clock was ticking and they hadn't gotten any closer to finding Tracie.

"I thought it strange that you—" he nodded toward Jacie "—would be talking to a man from the wrong side of town. What with you working out at the Big Elk with yer hotshot clients."

Zach stepped toward Sarly. "Get to the point."

Sarly glared at Zach. "Back off and I will." He faced Jacie, his features softening. "I had a sister once." He sighed. "The guy she was talkin' to was Juan Alvarez. I know that 'cause he used to work at the feed store with Henry Franks. Franks fired him when he didn't show up for two days. What with all the traffickin' goin' on round here, he figured Juan was involved, and Henry didn't want no part of that."

"Juan Alvarez." Jacie glanced across at Zach. "I know who that is."

"Then let's go." Zach was already off the porch

and halfway to the truck when he realized Jacie wasn't right behind him.

She stood on the porch with Mr. Sarly, shaking his hand and smiling. "Thank you, Mr. Sarly. You don't know how much I appreciate your help. If ever there's anything I can do for you, let me know."

His ruddy older face reddened even more. "Well, now. Next time you come bring ol' Mo some of whatever you brought this time. He seemed to like it right plenty."

Jacie patted Bull's hand and hurried toward the truck, climbing in without a word.

As they pulled away, Zach glanced in his mirror at the man retrieving his shotgun.

Zach's first instinct was to slam his foot to the accelerator. But the man just held it in one hand, patted the dog with the other and watched as they pulled out of sight.

The truck bumped along the rutted track to the highway, where Zach stopped and turned toward Jacie. "Where to?"

"The south side of Wild Oak Canyon. From what I know, Juan lives in a not-so-safe neighborhood on the edge of town. You'll want to make sure your gun is loaded and you're ready to fire."

Chapter Eight

Jacie's heart raced as they sped toward town. "Is this what FBI agents do? Follow clues, one step at a time to find a missing person or apprehend a suspect?"

"Yes."

Her hands twisted in her lap as she studied Zach, hoping to catch a glimpse of the former agent in him. Perhaps that would help her to understand what drew her sister to join the FBI. "Doesn't it get tedious and frustrating?"

"Yes." The word was short, with no telltale expression or anything a person could read in to.

Jacie frowned. "Anyone ever tell you that you don't talk much?"

His lips twitched. "Yes."

Jacie's stomach flipped. When he wasn't looking all fierce and deadly, the man was downright handsome.

"Are you always so forceful when you question people?" she pressed.

The hint of a smile disappeared. "Only when I'm out of time and patience."

A heavy weight pressed down on Jacie's shoulders. "Do you think we'll be too late?"

His foot lifted from the accelerator and he stared across at Jacie, his lips thin, his eyes narrowed. "No." Then he jammed his boot on the gas and the truck shot forward, faster than before. "At this point, we go all or nothing. Doubt can't be a factor. Got that?" He shot a stern frown at her, his nostrils flaring.

"You're right. My mother used to tell us not to borrow trouble." She sat back, the intensity of his stare making her glad he was on her side.

They blew into town, exceeding the speed limits, but Jacie didn't care.

"Turn left at the next street," she said.

Zach took the corner a little too fast. The bed of the truck skidded around behind them, leaving a trail of rubber in the hot pavement.

They passed houses along the road, the exteriors diminishing in care and upkeep the closer they got to the edge of town, until all that was left was a smattering of crumbling shacks and even seedier mobile homes.

"Next right." Jacie pulled her cowboy hat low on her forehead and tucked her hair beneath.

Zach nodded his approval. "You're learning."

Men sat on porches or lounged in old lawn

chairs; some stood around the shade trees. A small child played in the dirt, his hair shaggy, his clothes unkempt.

As Zach passed, narrowed gazes followed the shiny pickup's progress.

Jacie squirmed at the attention, not at all comfortable. "Is it safe to stop here?"

"If Juan is here, we need to find him. Safe or not. Maybe I should take you back to the Big Elk before I conduct business."

"No." Jacie sat up straighter. "I'm not afraid for myself."

Zach's lips twisted. "Don't tell me you're afraid for me?"

She shrugged. "Maybe." She was, but she wouldn't admit it. The man had a death wish, based on the way he walked up to Mr. Sarly, an angry bully holding a gun, as if he had nine lives to spare.

A young, dark-haired, dark-skinned man stepped out on the metal stairs leading into a ramshackle mobile home.

Jacie's heart fluttered. "That's him." She nodded toward the trailer. "That's Juan." She recognized him from one of her trips to Cara Jo's Diner.

"Let me do the talking and stay in the truck with the doors locked."

"No way." Jacie reached for the door handle. "You can't go out there alone. You need backup."

He snorted. "Like you're my backup? Please."

Anger bubbled up in Jacie's veins. "Some backup is better than none."

Zach grasped her hand in a tight clamplike hold. "Just do it. If I'm worrying about you, I might not see what's coming, like a fist or a bullet."

Jacie let go of the door handle and bit her bottom lip, torn between wanting to help and hurting the situation. "What are you going to do?"

"I'm going to ad-lib and get some information."

ZACH PULLED IN front of the trailer, shot the truck into park and climbed down. "Alvarez," he called out.

Alvarez leaned against the door of his trailer. "Lost, *gringo?*"

"You owe me and I'm here to collect." Zach marched toward the Hispanic.

Juan's eyes narrowed. "I don't owe you nothin'. Never saw you before."

A couple of the men who'd been lounging against beat-up cars pushed away and ambled toward Alvarez and the ruckus Zach was stirring.

"I asked for good stuff and you gave me shit." Zach marched up to the steps. "I want what I paid for, and I want it now."

Alvarez leaped to the ground and flipped out a switchblade. "I don't know who the hell you are, but I don't owe you nothin'."

Before the other two men could get close enough, Zach whispered low and without moving his lips, "You spoke to a woman two days ago in front of the diner."

Alvarez froze.

Zach went on. "I need to know what you said. Come with me and you won't be hurt." Louder he said, "Do I have to beat my stuff out of you?"

Juan lunged, his knife aimed at Zach's heart.

Zach ducked, grabbed Juan's knife hand and twisted it up and behind the man, pushing it high between his shoulder blades.

"Dios!" The knife fell from Juan's grip. "It's not here. I'll take you there, just don't break my arm."

"That's more like it." Without loosening his grip, Zach scooped up the knife and held it to Alvarez's throat. "Now tell your *compadres* to back off or I use this on you. And I warn you, *entiendo español." I understand Spanish.

Juan spoke to the men in rapid-fire Spanish.

Zach understood enough of the language to gather that Juan told his buddies he'd be okay, not to interfere, he'd take care of this.

With Juan as his shield, Zach moved toward the pickup.

Inside, Jacie unlocked the door and slid to the center.

Zach pulled his pistol from his shoulder holster

and handed it to her. "Point this at him and shoot if he so much as breathes wrong."

"Will do." She aimed the gun at Juan.

"In the truck," Zach ordered.

When Juan glanced into the truck, Jacie raised her head and stared straight into his eyes.

For a moment, Juan's eyes widened and he blinked. Then he ducked his head and climbed in without further argument.

Zach slammed the door shut, then rounded the truck and climbed into the driver's seat. "Just so you know, she's actually a better shot than I am, so do yourself a favor and behave."

Juan sat silent, staring at the pistol Jacie held in both hands, her finger caressing the trigger grip.

Back through town, Zach drove, his attention alternating between the road ahead, the rearview mirror and the woman holding the gun on the man beside her.

She held it steady, her face a mask of intensity.

Once he was certain he hadn't been followed, Zach shot out into the country, far enough away from town he could be certain no one was behind him.

Juan nodded toward the pistol in Jacie's hand. "She can put that down. I won't try to run or hurt you."

"If it's all the same to you, I'll keep it right here," she said.

Zach's chest swelled at her calm, clear and determined tones. She wasn't shaking, she hadn't hesitated to take the weapon and she probably was a better shot than he was, given that she hunted for a living.

Zach pulled off onto a side road and traveled another quarter of a mile before he parked beside a large clump of prickly pear cactus.

"How do you know my sister?" Jacie started.

"I don't know you and I don't know your sister," Juan muttered. "And I don't have your stuff, because I never sold you none."

Zach nodded to Jacie. "Keep the gun on him." Then he got out of the truck and rounded the front.

"You better answer our questions. My friend gets really cranky when he has to use force," Jacie warned, loud enough Zach could hear her.

He almost smiled, but that wouldn't be effective in what he planned next for Juan Alvarez.

Zach yanked open the passenger door.

"I don't know nothin'," Juan insisted.

"Maybe I can jog your memory a little." Zach grabbed Juan by the collar of his shirt and yanked him out onto the ground, then slammed him against the truck. "The woman you spoke to the day before yesterday was kidnapped last night. Which I suspect you already knew."

Juan shook his head but didn't voice a denial.

"Think real hard before you deny it. Next I will

use that pretty little gun my assistant is holding to blow each one of your fingers off, one at a time."

Jacie slid down out of the truck, her eyebrows raised. "He's not kidding. But if you want to play Russian roulette with your hands, we can oblige." She lifted the nine-millimeter pistol. "I want my sister back and I'll do anything to get her."

Juan's eyes bulged. "La Familia Diablos *es muy loco*. They'll kill me if they know I said anything."

"So, were you the one to set my sister up to take the fall in Wild Horse Canyon?" Jacie stepped closer. "Maybe I'll start with the trigger finger. Hold it out."

Zach's chest swelled even more at Jacie's ability to follow his lead. He knew without a doubt that she would never shoot another living being without deadly provocation, but Juan didn't know that.

Jacie was so convincing at her roll, Zach could almost believe she would start shooting. Zach shoved Juan to the ground and stepped on his hand, splaying the fingers wide. "What did you tell the woman?"

"I'll tell you whatever you want to know," Juan squealed. "Just don't shoot."

"Start talking." Jacie squatted next to the man.

"She got my name from my cousin in San Antonio. She came to me asking when a shipment was going down with the men from the DEA. She paid me five hundred dollars and promised not to tell La Familia who told her. That's all. Now are you going to let me up?"

Zach snorted. "I'll think about it."

"I didn't do anything," Juan insisted.

"Did you inform La Familia Diablos that my sister was coming?"

"No. I hate La Familia. They killed my brother, Roberto. I owe them no allegiance."

"Let him up," Jacie demanded.

Zach removed his foot from the man's hand, grabbed his shoulder and hauled him to his feet. "Don't try anything," he warned Juan.

Jacie's eyebrows furrowed. "You knew the woman you'd spoken to was captured?"

"Sí."

Her gaze narrowed. "How?"

He shrugged, rubbing at the hand Zach had stood on. "News travels fast in the barrio."

"Then you also know Los Lobos killed the men who captured her and took her."

Juan's lips clamped shut and he stared from Zach to Jacie.

"Maybe you even know where Los Lobos are keeping her?" Jacie prompted.

"No." Juan looked away.

"Liar." Zach's lips thinned and he stepped toward Juan, fists clenched. "Either you know or you know someone who does." He held out his hand for the gun Jacie still held. She slapped it into his open palm.

Zach's fingers curled around the handle, warm from Jacie's touch. "Save us the crap and tell us what you do know."

Juan stared from Jacie back to Zach. "You aren't going to shoot me." He straightened his shoulders. "You don't have it in you."

"Try me," Zach said, his tone, low and dangerous. His hand rose with the gun pointed at Juan's forehead.

Juan stared down the barrel. At first Zach thought he would succeed at calling his bluff. To hell with that.

Zach pointed the nine-millimeter at Juan's foot and fired off a round.

"Madre de Dios!" Juan grabbed his foot and hopped in place before he fell to the ground and pulled off his shoe. Blood oozed from the side of his foot. "You shot me!"

Jacie stood with her mouth hanging open. Then she swallowed hard, her throat working in spasms. She shook back her hair and stared down her nose at the wounded man. "A flesh wound. The next one will count." She held out her hand. "My turn."

Zach passed the weapon back to her, his eyebrows rising.

"Did I mention I'll do just about anything to get my sister back alive?" She aimed the gun at

Juan's kneecap. "I want answers now, not after she's dead."

Juan held his hands over the knee, as if they would have any effect stopping a bullet. "They'll kill me."

Jacie shrugged. "Us or them? You choose."

"Okay, okay." Juan stood. "Los Lobos might have taken her into one of the caves they use to stage drug runs. In Wild Horse Canyon."

"Guess who's taking us on a little trip into the canyon?" Zach's mouth quirked upward.

Juan's eyes rounded into saucers. "No. I told you what you wanted to know. Let me go."

"Sorry. That's not an option." Zach nodded to Jacie. "Let's go. We're burning daylight." The quicker they got to the canyon, the better for Tracie. Even a trained agent didn't hold up well under torture.

Zach shoved Juan into the truck.

Jacie got in beside their captive and took Zach's gun from him.

Without uttering another word, Zach slid into the driver's seat and spun the truck around, heading toward Hank's Raging Bull Ranch.

When he passed the turnoff to the Big Elk, Jacie looked at him with a frown. "Shouldn't we go back to the Big Elk and get horses?"

"Shouldn't you take me back to *mi casa?*" Juan whined.

"No," Zach answered. "You'll be showing us exactly where this cave is."

Juan pointed at his foot. "But I'm injured. I can't walk."

"You'll be on horseback," Zach said.

Juan didn't look any happier. "I don't know how to ride."

"Can I just shoot him now?" Jacie asked.

Juan sat in silence for a moment, glaring out the front windshield. "What if I don't remember?"

"Then we'll shoot your knees and leave you out there for the four-legged coyotes to clean up." Jacie waved the gun. "Enough excuses."

Zach fought the smile. Jacie was getting into her tough-girl role, maybe a little too much. She was tough, but Zach knew the real woman beneath the attitude. She wouldn't shoot.

Zach, on the other hand, wouldn't suffer a stubborn fool. If the man knew something, Zach would shoot one digit at a time until he got the information out of him. He wouldn't let Tracie go through what Toni had suffered. Not if he could help it.

He drove the rest of the way to the Raging Bull without speaking another word, his mind running through the task at hand. Hopefully, the FBI and DEA would prove some kind of help storming the cave. Zach couldn't do it on his own. Not as heavily fortified as the Los Lobos had proved by shooting down the helicopter. Assuming the Los Lobos had done the shooting.

An operations tent had been set up in a field beside the barn on the Raging Bull Ranch. A phalanx of rental cars and dark SUVs lined the fence railing, where people milled about, pressing hand-held radios to their ears.

Zach pulled into the front drive, weaving through the cars to find a place to park among the government vehicles.

Hank met them with a frown denting his forehead. "Glad you made it."

Jacie let herself out of her side of the truck. She handed Zach the gun. "I think he'll behave as long as he's surrounded."

Zach took the Glock. "Thanks." Then he turned to Hank. "What's the latest?"

"The FBI and DEA have joined forces in the search and rescue efforts. They have boots on the ground and birds in the air in Wild Horse Canyon, tracking from the point where you found the four-by-four and the dead members of La Familia."

Jacie stepped up to Hank. "Any sign of my sister?"

Hank shook his head. "Sorry. None."

Her shoulders sagged for a moment, then she

straightened and turned to Zach. "Well, then, what are we waiting for?"

Hank stared from Zach to Jacie and then to the man standing behind them. "You two find out something?"

"Yeah." Zach jerked his head toward their informant. "This is the man who told Tracie about the op going down in the canyon."

Hank's eyebrows dipped. "What's he doing here?"

"He knows where the Los Lobos hole up in a cave in the canyon when they're making a drug run." Zach gave the informant a pointed look. "He's going to show us where that is."

Juan grumbled, "If I don't, you'll blow my knees off."

Hank laughed and pounded Zach on the back. "A man after my own heart."

"Not man." Zach jerked his head toward Jacie. "Woman. She's the one who threatened to blow his knees apart and, what was it you said?"

"Leave me for the four-legged coyotes to finish off." Juan glared at Jacie. "She's an animal."

Jacie shrugged and repeated her mantra. "I want my sister back."

Hank hooked Zach's elbow and he led him away from Juan. "Are you going to let the operations center know what you found?"

Zach sucked in a breath and let it out. "I don't know."

Jacie joined them. "Don't. We don't know who is bad in the group, possibly in both agencies, given the two DEA agents weren't on orders."

"Probably a wise decision." Hank nodded. "However, going up against Los Lobos alone is suicide."

"Not if they don't see you." Zach glanced at Jacie. "Which means I can't allow you to go."

"Like hell you can't." Jacie stuck a finger into his chest. "Look, mister, that's my sister out there. I'm going to get her back. And I know those canyons better than any of you."

"I'll have to trust our friend there to get me in and out at night. I'm sure he's had practice."

"You're waiting until dark?" Jacie asked.

"Can't go any sooner without alerting Los Lobos and the team of rescuers." Zach glanced toward the western sky, where the sun made its way toward the horizon. It would be dark before long and the air rescue units would be called in, as would the ground teams.

"Are you sure you don't want to let the FBI and DEA know what we found out?" Hank asked.

Zach raised his eyebrows. "What exactly do we know?"

"Los Lobos have a cave hideout in the canyon,"

Jacie offered. "Not that I'm condoning asking for FBI or DEA help on this."

"Do we know for certain they do or is Juan leading us on?" Zach shot back at her.

Jacie swallowed hard on a rising knot forming around her vocal cords. "My sister might be in that cave."

"If she is, we'll need more than just you and me to bring her out. We need to recon and see what we're up against."

"Right." Jacie's back stiffened. "You said 'we.'"

"I really meant me." Zach pointed at the Hispanic lounging against his truck. "Juan is only showing me where. I'd go it alone if I knew where. As it is, I don't trust Juan any farther than I can throw him."

"All the more reason to take me," Jacie insisted. "I can watch your back."

Hank laid a hand on Jacie's arm. "Zach's right."

"Oh, please, you can't take sides. You put him on this case to help me, not replace me."

"He's trained to do this stuff. You'll only—"

Jacie held up her hand. "Slow him down, right? And what do you expect me to do while you go fight the terrorists? Stay home and knit?" She waved at her dusty clothes. "I'm not the stay-at-home kinda gal, in case you haven't noticed."

Zach grinned. "No, you're not." His smile died. "You can stay and lurk around the operations tent with the FBI and DEA and see what they've come up with," Hank suggested. "Maybe you can figure out who our mole is in the bureau."

Jacie snorted. "Like I'd have a clue."

Zach turned to Hank. "I'll need a couple horses."

"I'll have my foreman set you up. For now, get to the kitchen and grab a bite to eat. You might need it, if you get lost in the canyon."

"Good point. I'll be sure to take a flare with me."

Jacie stood with a frown drawing her eyebrows close, her arms crossed. "Glad you two can joke about this."

"Come on, you could use some food too." Zach hooked her arm and urged her toward the house, calling over his shoulder, "Juan."

Juan sneered at him.

"If you want food, join us."

For a moment Juan remained stubbornly leaning against the truck. Then he pushed away and followed in a deliberately slow swagger.

JACIE SAT THROUGH a meal quickly prepared by Hank's housekeeper. She could barely swallow, her throat muscles clenching each time she thought of her sister and how long she'd been held captive by notoriously vicious gangsters. She tried not to think about it, but her only other thoughts strayed to Zach and what he was about to undertake.

Riding horseback through the canyon was treacherous enough during the day. At night it was deadly. If Juan didn't know exactly where he was going, they could end up lost and another rescue mission for the local authorities.

As dusk descended, dread threatened to weigh Jacie down.

She walked with Zach and Juan to the barn and stood back as Zach tied a saddlebag loaded with provisions onto the back of his saddle.

Juan's gloomy countenance didn't help to ease Jacie's mind.

"Well, that's it." Zach patted the horse's hindquarters and led him toward the rear entrance to the barn.

Jacie walked alongside him, her head bent. "I don't like this."

"I know." Zach faced her and tipped her chin with his finger. "We'll do our best to locate your sister and get back here as quickly as possible. Maybe even before sunup."

"What if you get in trouble?" She stared into his face, wishing he'd reconsider and take her along. "What if you're hurt?"

He smiled, his hand cupping her cheek. "Worried about me?"

Jacie stiffened and had a retort ready on her lips, but stopped short of delivering it when she realized she was worried about him. "I haven't known you long, but damn it, I am worried about you. I kinda got used to having you around." Her hand covered the one he'd used to cup her cheek and she pulled it lower, pressing a kiss into his palm.

"Stay safe for me, will you?" His eyes dark in the dim lighting from the overhead bulbs, he leaned close and captured her lips in a soul-stealing kiss.

For what felt as long as a lifetime and as short as a moment at once, the world around Jacie faded away, leaving just her and Zach.

Their tongues connected, thrusting and caressing.

When Zach broke away, he smoothed his hand over her hair. "Stay here. I trust Hank to keep you safe."

She laughed, the sound lacking any humor. "I'm not the one who needs to worry about being safe."

Zach smiled, chucked her beneath her chin and strode out of the barn, leading his horse.

The men had agreed not to mount, but to lead their horses quietly away from the barn, walking close to the animals so as not to be spotted by the agencies working the case.

The activity at the operations tent increased with the search teams reporting in.

During all the confusion of agents and law enforcement personal converging, no one seemed to notice the two horses walking across the pasture. Eventually the two faded into the distance.

Jacie remained in the shadows, every nerve ending screaming for her to follow.

Chapter Nine

Hank appeared at Jacie's side. "I asked Ben Harding to accompany you until Zach returns from the canyon."

"Thanks, but I don't need a babysitter." Jacie glanced one last time into the darkness. "What I need is a ride back to the Big Elk Ranch. Zach didn't leave me his truck keys."

Hank shook his head. "Zach wanted you to stay here where you'll be safe."

"From what?" Jacie raised her hand. "I didn't get kidnapped. I'm not the one being tortured. No one is after me. Unless you know something I don't."

Hank smiled. "You and your sister are very much alike. When she came to me for help, she didn't mince words and didn't stand for any fluff." He patted her arm. "Ben should be here in less than fifteen minutes. As soon as he arrives, I'll have him take you back to the Big Elk."

"Thank you." Guilt forced Jacie to add, "I'm sorry I bit your head off."

Hank's smile disappeared. "I understand. It's hard to lose someone you love. Even harder to know that they might still be alive."

Jacie had heard about Hank's wife and son disappearing a couple of years before. She laid a hand on his arm. "Still nothing about your family?"

"Nothing."

"Mr. Derringer, Grant Lehmann's here to speak with you," Hank's foreman called out.

"If you'll excuse me. Lehmann's an old friend and a regional director of the FBI."

"Good, maybe he can get things moving on finding my sister."

Hank left her standing in the barn's rear doorway.

Jacie wandered over to the operations tent and peeked in.

Agents and sheriff's deputies were finishing up with their reports. Everyone said the same thing. No sign of Tracie Kosart, or anyone else for that matter. The ground-tracking team had followed the trail until it disappeared. They suspected the kidnappers knew enough to drag a branch or something from the back of their vehicles to smooth away their tire tracks.

"Stopping in?"

The voice behind her made Jacie jump. She spun to face Bruce Masterson, wearing black chinos, a black polo shirt and a headset looped over his head, currently pushed back from his ears.

He held out a hand, inviting her to precede him into the portable ops center. "You look so much like your sister it takes me aback every time I see you."

Jacie stepped beneath the lights strung out between tent poles before responding, "That happens with identical twins." She halted just inside and faced him, something gnawing at her since she'd first called him. "I have a question for you."

He grinned. "Shoot."

"You sounded surprised to hear that Tracie had come to see me. Why? I thought you two were living together." Jacie tilted her head to the side. "Wouldn't you know when she'd left and where she was headed? Or have your living arrangements changed since the engagement?"

The man shrugged. "She left without telling me. I assumed she was called out on a job."

"Were you two having a fight or anything?"

Bruce shook his head. "No. At least not one I was involved in."

"She didn't leave a note?"

"No. Her suitcase was gone, so I assumed she

was on assignment. It was too late to call the office and double-check." Bruce fiddled with the headset, staring over Jacie's shoulder. He waved at someone behind Jacie. "I have to admit I was a little worried, but happy to hear from you to know she was with you. Until you told me she'd been kidnapped. I had to beg to get special permission to join the search and rescue mission."

His answers sounded legit; still, Jacie couldn't imagine her organized sister taking off without informing her fiancé of her whereabouts. Jacie had opened her mouth to say just that when a voice called out her name. She turned, looking for the source.

Bruce glanced around the tent. "Where'd your boyfriend go?"

Jacie hesitated, the truth the first thing that wanted to pop out of her mouth. She bit down hard on her tongue and thought before answering. "He got called away on business."

"I thought I just saw him here. Isn't it late to be called in to work?"

"Apparently he didn't think so. He headed into…El Paso to find a business center."

"Is he coming back?"

"Um, yes. Of course." Jacie sent a silent prayer that what she'd said wasn't yet another untruth.

Zach would be back, and hopefully with news of her sister. In the meantime, she had to wait.

"What exactly does your boyfriend do?"

Irritation flared in Jacie. She didn't like lying, but Bruce's barrage of questions left her no choice. "I'm not exactly sure. I think he's into security work, something high-tech. When he talks about it, I glaze over."

She forced a fake smile. To handle the guilt, she told herself she was on an undercover mission and the lies were only to protect herself and her partner. Not that Zach considered himself her partner. Still, no one, other than herself and Hank, needed to know he was out scouting the canyon for the Los Lobos cave. Not even Tracie's fiancé, who for some reason Tracie hadn't seen fit to inform of her plans.

A man wearing a black cowboy hat ducked beneath the tent. "Jacie?" It had to be the guy Hank had promised, Ben Harding.

Jacie raised her hand, relieved she didn't have to answer any more of Bruce's questions. "I suppose that's my ride."

Bruce frowned. "Headed back to the Big Elk? And here I thought you'd stick around awhile."

"I'm of no use here."

"I wouldn't say that. It's like having Tracie here." Bruce slid a finger along Jacie's cheek. "You two are so much alike."

Jacie frowned. Zach had just touched her cheek

before he'd left, and this man was wiping away that warm fuzzy feeling she'd gotten the first time.

An icky sensation crept into Jacie's gut. Was Bruce coming on to her? She shook her head. No. She was reading too much into his touch and comment. "We're only alike physically. We're completely different when it comes to tastes, likes and dislikes." She added a little emphasis to the last statement as if telling Bruce *back off, you're not my type.*

The cowboy stepped through the crowd and stopped beside Jacie. "I take it you're Jacie?"

She gave him a tight smile, relieved he'd come to take her away. "That's me. Let's go." Jacie hooked his arm and led him out of the tent. Okay, if she was honest with herself, she dragged the unsuspecting man out.

Once outside in the darkness of night, Ben laughed. "Hey, what's the rush?"

"I'm not a secret agent and my sister's boyfriend was asking questions about Zach and where he was." She slowed to a stop and gave her rescuer a smile. "Sorry, that was rude of me." Jacie stuck out a hand. "I'm Jacie Kosart."

The cowboy removed his hat and took her hand. "Ben Harding. Nice to meet you. I understand I'm here to take over for Zach while he's busy."

Jacie's hand dropped to her side and she continued toward the makeshift parking lot. "No, you're just here to take me to the Big Elk Ranch, where I live."

"Oh, that's not what I had understood from Hank."

"Apparently Hank worries about the wrong people. Which vehicle did you drive?"

Still carrying his hat, Ben scratched his head. "Hank's a pretty smart guy. The dark gray pickup on the very end." He pointed to the one.

Jacie lengthened her stride, eager to be on her way before anyone waylaid her with unwanted questions. "Maybe so, but I'm not the one who's missing. I don't need a babysitter and I told him as much."

Ben chuckled. "Okay, then. Let's get you home."

"Thank you." Jacie climbed into the passenger seat and leaned back, her mind miles away from the interior of the truck, far across the Texas landscape, near the edge of the canyon with Zach and Juan. She hoped Zach kept a close eye on his informant.

Jacie hadn't trusted the guy and worried he'd try something, injuring Zach or setting him up to take a fall with Los Lobos.

Ben drove the length of the Raging Bull Ranch driveway before speaking again. "Which way?"

Jacie gave him the directions.

"Hank tells me it's your sister lost in the canyon. I'm sorry."

"Not lost...kidnapped."

"Right." Ben nodded. "I don't know much about Zach, but from what I've learned about Hank, he's a good judge of character. If he's assigned Zach to help find your sister, I'm sure he'll get the job done."

"Thanks. I just wish he'd taken me."

"Hank says you work as a trail guide at the Big Elk. I can see where that would come in handy out in the canyon. Why didn't he take you?"

"Zach gave me some crap about stealth. I think he's crazy going in alone."

"He's trained as an FBI agent. He knows the risks. And from what I've heard, he's not afraid to take them."

"As long as he doesn't get himself killed."

"There is that." Ben glanced across at her, his eyes reflecting the light from the dash. "He knows the stakes and he signed on anyway. I guess most FBI or law enforcement types understand there's always a chance you might not make it back from a mission."

Jacie sat up straighter. "Not helping."

Ben chuckled. "Sorry. I forgot your sister was—is—FBI."

"Yeah, she is and I'm not." Jacie turned sideways, facing Ben. "What is it that drives someone into a job like that? Are they adrenaline junkies or something?"

Ben shook his head, his gaze on the highway in front of him. "Maybe for some. For most, it's a need to fight for truth and justice."

Jacie snorted. "At the risk of your own life?"

His gaze captured hers for a moment. "Don't tell me you wouldn't give your life for your sister."

"In a heartbeat. But she's not giving her life for me, she's sacrificing it for nameless, faceless people."

"No, she's sacrificing for the good of a lot of people. What about for the next child that could be molested if she didn't fight to get the child molester off the streets? Or the families with small children or young teens that live in terror while a serial killer stalks their neighborhood? Those people have faces. They are real."

Jacie slumped in her seat. "You're right. I'm just mad she didn't tell me everything when she came out here to supposedly visit. Now she's got herself in a bind and Zach could well be walking into a trap." She flung out her hands. "I hate not knowing and not doing anything."

"Understandable. Just have faith he'll be okay and we'll find your sister."

Jacie couldn't leave it up to faith. She was a doer. By the time they arrived at the Big Elk Ranch, she'd worked herself up into a silent lather. No sooner had Ben pulled up in the parking lot of the lodge than she was out of the truck. "No need to stay, I'm just going to wait in my cabin until I hear from Zach or my sister."

Ben's brow furrowed. "If you're sure you'll be all right?"

"I will." She waved. "Thanks, Ben." Then she slammed the door and took off for her cabin. Wait in her cabin, ha!

She waited as long as it took for Ben to back up, turn around and head back the way he'd come, before she made a sharp turn toward the barn.

"Jacie?" Richard Giddings called out from the front porch of the lodge. "Is that you?"

Jacie swallowed her irritation and answered, "Yes, sir."

"What's been happening? I haven't seen or heard from you since this morning."

"Rich, I don't have time to fill you in. I need to get back out there."

He dropped down off the porch. "Out where?"

"The canyon."

"At night?" Her boss shook his head and looked around her. "That's insane. Where's Zach?"

The secrecy of the mission Zach was on required Jacie to keep the truth from her boss, but she didn't have to lie. "He had business to attend to."

"All the more reason for you to stay put. No one in their right mind should be out in that canyon at night."

Jacie stopped herself from snorting out loud. She couldn't agree with him more, but she also wasn't at liberty to say why. Not that she didn't trust Richard with her life and that of her sister, but what if someone overheard their conversation? Someone who would inform Los Lobos they had a visitor on his way to spy on them?

"Tracie's been gone over twenty-four hours."

Richard pulled her into a big bear hug. "Then come up to the lodge and stay with me until Zach gets back."

She considered it. But she'd rather go out to the canyon and follow Zach.

"No, you're not going out to the canyon tonight. I won't allow you to make use of any of the Big Elk assets to commit suicide." Richard set her at arm's length.

She stared up at him. "How do you know what I'm thinking?"

"As long as you've been working here, I think I'd know you by now. You're a doer and it's eating you up not to be doin'." He slung one arm over her shoulders. "Now, are you coming to the lodge for a beer or going to your cabin to wait?"

"Thanks for the offer, but I think I'll sit it out in my cabin. I could use a shower."

"Have it your way, but the offer remains open. I'm here if you need a shoulder."

"Thanks." Tears lodged in Jacie's throat. This

man had been more than good to her. He'd been the father she missed so badly, the friend she'd needed on more than one occasion. Jacie tamped down the urge to ride off into the canyon and did as Ben had suggested and had faith that Zach would return unharmed. And with news of her sister.

Jacie trudged toward her cottage. A quick glance behind her confirmed Richard remained where she'd left him, watching her as she made her way home.

Once inside, she went through the motions of stripping off her dirty clothes. In the corner, her sister's suitcase lay on its side, just as she'd left it over a day ago.

Jacie dropped to her haunches and unzipped the case, feeling like a sneak looking through her sister's things. Maybe buried among Tracie's pajamas and blue jeans, she'd find a clue that would help her understand why she'd left Bruce without telling him and what she thought she'd find following the DEA agents into the canyon.

The suitcase was just like Tracie, neat and organized, each T-shirt folded precisely the same, the socks rolled military-style, a habit probably learned at Quantico.

Jacie unzipped a side pouch inside the suitcase and found Tracie's wallet with her FBI identification and her cell phone.

Her heartbeat picking up, Jacie recalled Cara Jo saying something about Tracie staring at her phone the whole time she'd been in the diner. Had she tried to call Bruce and he hadn't answered? Or had she been calling another contact to verify whatever she'd found?

Jacie hit the on button and waited. The screen flickered to life; a battery with a red line blinked into view. Great. Low battery. The screen warning cleared, replaced by another screen requiring a four-digit pass code.

Stumped, Jacie stared at the little boxes and rows of numbers. What would Tracie have used? She keyed in the month and day of Tracie's birthday. That didn't open it. She keyed in the month and year. Another failed attempt. The little battery indicator in the top corner indicated eleven percent.

Her heart racing, Jacie dug through her sister's belongings, searching for her phone charger. When she didn't find one, she slipped on her shirt and jeans, grabbed Tracie's car keys and ran out to the little economy car she'd driven up from San Antonio. Surely she had a charger in the car.

Once again, she struck out and her own cell phone charger didn't work on her sister's model. When Jacie emerged from the little car, she trudged back to the house. She probably only had a few more tries before either the phone locked up or the battery died.

As she stepped up on the porch, the sound of gravel shifting brought her out of her intense concentration on her sister's phone, and Jacie glanced around.

The moon shone down on the lodge and cabins, casting long shadows at the corners and sides.

Jacie listened for the sound again. Perhaps a raccoon was on its way through to the barn to get into the feed, or one of the ranch dogs had scampered into the shadows. With a shrug, Jacie entered the cottage quickly and closed the door, locking it behind her. Never had she felt unsafe at the Big Elk Ranch. All this cloak-and-dagger stuff had her spooked and she found herself wishing Zach was there with her.

How could one man become so much a part of her life in so short a time? Jacie stared at her sister's cell phone she'd laid on the bed. Maybe she'd think of the code while shampooing the dirt out of her hair.

Once again, she slipped out of her clothes, grabbed a towel out of the linen closet of the tiny cabin and stepped into the closet-sized bathroom. At least the bathtub was a normal size. Opting for a bath instead of a shower, she filled the tub and added some of the bath salts Tracie had given her for Christmas. She realized this was the first time she'd used them and she wanted to cry.

When the tub was full, she sank into the steamy water, sliding low to immerse her hair. She came up, blinking water from her eyes, and squirted a healthy dose of shampoo into her hand. Jacie went to work washing away the dust from her nearly fatal helicopter ride of earlier that day. Had it only been that morning? So much had happened since then. And yet so little.

Jacie slipped beneath the surface again, rinsing the bubbles out of her hair. A dull thump sounded through the bathtub water.

She sat up straight, water splashing over the edge of the tub, her ears perked.

A soft scraping sound reached her ears and sent her flying out of the tub, wrapping a towel around her middle as she emerged from the bathroom. "Who's there?"

The scraping had stopped and nothing but an eerie silence surrounded Jacie. She reached for the nine-millimeter Glock she kept in her nightstand, fully loaded.

"I have a gun and I know how to use it," she called out. Normally she'd feel silly about saying that out loud. But nothing about the past two days had been normal. A shiver rippled down her spine.

She rushed through the little cabin, turning off the lights. If someone was out there, he wouldn't be able to see a shadow moving around inside, and she might possibly see his figure moving around the outside. Jacie dressed in clean work clothes instead of her pajamas.

Unable to sleep and seriously afraid, she pulled the mattress off the bed and laid it on the floor, then wrapped her mother's quilt around her body. Propping her back against the wall, she pointed her gun at the only door into and out of the house. She waited for morning and the return of Zach and her sanity.

Chapter Ten

Zach forced Juan to take the lead as they found their way through the twists and turns of the canyon. The horses picked their way carefully over stones and around boulders, sliding in some places.

By the light of a near-full moon, Zach studied the walls, rock formations and crevices, memorizing them in case he ended up finding his way out of the maze on his own.

He still wasn't sure Juan knew where he was going or if the man was leading him straight into a trap. Without much else to go on, Zach had to take his chances.

The crevices narrowed and widened, but they were always wide and cleared enough to allow a four-wheel-drive ATV access.

After they had traveled for nearly an hour, the walls loomed higher, the path narrowed and the shadows made it more difficult to see.

Zach shifted in his saddle to ease the aching

muscles of his inner thighs and give his sore tailbone a break. Hopefully they'd get there soon. He didn't know how effective he would be if he was too stiff to climb off his horse.

Juan halted his gelding at a giant outcropping of boulders and dismounted.

Zach rode up beside him. "Why are you stopping?" he asked, careful to keep his voice low. Sound bounced off the canyon walls, echoing up and down the length.

"This is as far as I go on horseback." He tugged his horse to the side, into the deepest shadows.

"How much farther ahead is it?" Zach dismounted as well.

"I will show you. But we'll go on foot. The horses will make too much noise and alert the lookouts."

Zach tied his horse to a stunted tree, wedged in the crevice between giant boulders. Juan did the same, then led Zach around the outcropping, hugging the shadows along the base of the canyon walls.

They'd gone the equivalent of four football fields when Juan stopped and pointed to a dark spot ahead and on the left. "That's the cave and this is as far as I go."

Zach studied the location, the possible areas he could use as cover and concealment. "Okay." He nodded.

"I've done what you asked. Now you can let me go, no?"

Zach shook his head. "Sorry, buddy. I want to make sure you didn't lead me on a wild-goose chase, *and* I can't risk you alerting the gang in the cave. You get to stay here and wait for me to return."

Zach pulled a wad of zip-ties from his back pocket, grabbed Juan's wrist and whipped it up and behind him. He grabbed the man's other hand and slipped the zip-tie around Juan's wrists, tugging it tight.

"What are you doing?" Juan danced around, tugging his hands against the bindings. "You can't leave me here tied up. I am not a member of Los Lobos. If they knew I led you to them, they would kill me."

"Then you better keep really quiet so they don't find you. When I get back, I'll cut the ties and we'll mosey on home." Zach crossed his arms. "Now, are you going to sit so that I can bind your legs, or do I have to knock you down?"

Juan shook his head. "I promise I won't go anywhere."

"Since I don't know you well enough to stake my life on your word, you'll have to go with the zip-ties. I figure it'll take you at least as long as it takes me to get up there and back to find a rock to break them on."

"What about coyotes and snakes? Look, amigo, don't leave me like this."

"You'll be okay for the short time I'm gone." He pointed to the ground. "Sit."

With his hands tied behind him, Juan sighed and dropped to his knees and then to his butt, kicking his feet out in front of him. "You're one tough hombre. If I had my knife…"

"But you don't, and I might have some discussions with you if this is all a waste of my time." Zach slipped the plastic strap around Juan's ankles. Then he pulled a small roll of duct tape from his other back pocket and slapped a piece over Juan's mouth.

With his guide secured from running away or running his mouth, Zach proceeded around the bend and along the base of the canyon toward the dark shadow that was the mouth of a cave. He didn't hurry, careful not to scuff gravel or trip over unseen rocks. When he came within twenty yards of the entrance, he stopped and scoped the surrounding area. So far he hadn't sighted a single guard. Nothing and no one moved in and out of the cave or anywhere else around it.

Zach held his weapon in front of him. From where he stood to the entrance, there were no shadows to hug, no boulders to dive behind. He'd have to make a mad dash in case a sniper spotted him and started taking potshots at him.

With a deep breath, Zach ran toward the entrance, zigzagging so that he didn't provide an easy target for someone who could halfway shoot a gun.

He climbed a rise and ducked into the cave, slipping into the shadows. Deeper inside, a single light illuminated a small area. Having met no resistance, Zach took the time to let his eyes adjust to the limited lighting before he moved closer to the glow. Voices carried to him, and by the sound of them, they were in Spanish.

Two men sat in front of a fire, one holding a stick at the end of which was some dead, skinned animal, roasting in the flame. The other smoked a cigarette. Both men had weapons, but they lay on the ground beside them. Apparently they weren't expecting company or anyone else.

Besides the men and the fire, there were small wooden crates and cardboard boxes lining the walls. Zach passed one after the other. Most of them were empty.

As he neared the fire, one of the men spoke in rapid-fire Spanish telling a raucous story about a woman and her mother. The other burst out laughing.

Zach stepped forward, his weapon drawn. In Spanish he asked, "Are you Los Lobos?"

The men reached for their weapons.

Still speaking in Spanish, Zach warned, "Reach for your guns and I'll shoot you. Hands up."

One man looked at the other and dove for his gun.

Zach shot him in the shoulder, knocking him backward into a wall.

The man grabbed his shoulder and slid to the ground, moaning.

"Don't shoot," the other man said in halting English. He kicked both weapons toward Zach, his hands still in the air.

"Are you Los Lobos?"

"No."

Zach pointed at the downed man's other shoulder. "No lies."

The bleeding man raised his good, bloodied hand. "*Sí, señor.* We are Los Lobos."

"Where is the woman?" Zach asked.

Both men looked at each other, their foreheads wrinkled in frowns.

The man who was still standing shook his head. "What woman?"

"The one the Los Lobos murdered two La Familia Diablos guys to get."

Again the standing man shook his head. "Los Lobos didn't take a woman. With the FBI and DEA all over the canyon, we couldn't leave our stuff here. The boss had us move it. We stayed to clean up the last of it." He blinked, glancing over Zach's shoulder.

Before Zach could spin, a hard poke in his back made him think twice.

"Drop your gun," a heavily accented voice demanded.

Zach had no intention of giving up his weapon. In a lightning-fast move, he ducked to the side and knocked the barrel of the rifle the man held downward, causing the stock to lever up and hit his attacker in the jaw.

The man pulled the trigger and a bullet ricocheted off the floor, disappearing into the shadows.

The unarmed men dropped to the ground.

Zach jerked the rifle out of the man's hands and pressed his Glock into the guy's cheek. "Are there any more of you hiding or coming?"

The man with the gun in his cheek shook his head, his eyes wide. *"No comprende."*

The other man translated and received a response in Spanish. The translator faced Zach. "There are two more on their way to help move the rest of the stuff."

"Then let's get down to business." Zach nudged the gun deeper into the man's face. "Where's the woman?"

A thin sheen of sweat broke out on the man's

face and he fired off his answer in such garbled Spanish Zach couldn't make heads or tails of it.

"What did he say?" Zach demanded of the translator.

"Los Lobos didn't take the woman. La Familia Diablos did."

Zach shook his head. "Then Los Lobos killed the two Diablos who took her, and now Los Lobos has her."

The man with the gun in his cheek shook his head and rattled off more Spanish.

"That is not the truth, *señor*. La Familia still has her. Someone made it look like Los Lobos killed those men."

"How about I shoot one of you at a time until someone tells me the truth?" Zach said.

All three men held up their hands. The man who understood English best spoke. "We are telling you the truth. Ramon just returned to pick us up. News from the boss is La Familia Diablos set it up to look like Los Lobos took the woman so that the Federales would look in the wrong place for her and cause troubles for Los Lobos."

For a long moment Zach continued to hold his weapon to the man's cheek. In his gut he knew what they were saying was most likely the truth. Finally he eased away from the trio, backing toward the cave entrance. He scooped up the other two weapons and slung all three over his shoulder while still holding the Glock on them.

"I'll let you live this time. Believe me when I say, if what you've told me is all lies, I'll find you and I'll rip your limbs off one at a time and make you wish you were dead long before you are."

Without waiting for them to respond, Zach slipped out of the cave and ran back across the wide-open space, weighed down by the three extra guns. When he reached the relative safety of a large boulder, he removed the bolts from the Los Lobos rifles and tossed the weapons on the ground.

A shout sounded behind him. He leaned around the boulder. The three men emerged from the cave, headed in his direction.

Zach fired off a round, kicking up the rocks at their feet. They hurried back to the cave entrance.

With no more time to play around, Zach ran back to where he'd left Juan. With Juan's switchblade, he severed the zip-ties. "Let's go."

Juan ripped the tape off his mouth. "Did you find the woman?"

"No. If you want to live, you'll get moving." Zach didn't wait for Juan; he ran back the way they'd come, reaching the horses before Juan.

The sound of engines revving echoed off the canyon walls as Zach and Juan mounted the horses.

Now that he knew that most of Los Lobos had

vacated the canyon, Zach wasn't as concerned about noise as he was about getting a bullet in his back. He urged his horse to a trot, praying the animal wouldn't break a leg on the rocky terrain. They maneuvered through the maze of canyon corridors until they emerged at the base of the ridge where Tracie had been taken.

AFTER SITTING IN the dark on the floor for what felt like an hour, Jacie glanced at the clock. Thirty minutes? It had only been thirty minutes? That's it? She refused to wait around her cabin another moment. She had to get back out to the canyon. Zach could be in trouble. Maybe he'd found Tracie and they were fighting their way out and needed an extra gun to even the odds.

Jacie dressed in clean black jeans, a black T-shirt and her black leather jacket. She knotted her long hair in a rubber band and shoved it under a black baseball cap Richard had given her. After loading her rifle and her Glock with rounds, she shoved a box of bullets in each jacket pocket and shoved the chair away from the door.

If someone was out there, she was loaded and wouldn't hesitate to shoot. She switched on the porch light and flung open the door.

The porch was empty and nothing moved as far as she could see into the shadows past the illumination. When she turned to lock the door, she noticed that the oil-rubbed bronze door lock had fresh scratches in it.

Her gut tightened. Someone had definitely been trying to get in. On instinct, she went back inside, closed the door and grabbed her sister's credentials and cell phone. She shoved them beneath a plastic bag of moldy tomatoes in the bottom of her miniature refrigerator. No one would bother them there.

Having hidden the only two things she considered of any interest to anyone, she locked the front door and slipped across the compound to the barn, weapon drawn and ready.

Once inside the barn, she fumbled in the tack room for a flashlight, switching it on and shining the light around the interior for good measure. She'd had that creepy, being-watched feeling since she'd come back to the Big Elk.

Satisfied she was alone, she led D'Artagnan, her bay gelding, from his stall and tossed a saddle over his back. Once she had the saddle cinched and the bridle settled over the horse's head, she turned to lead him out the back of the barn.

A hinge squeaked and the overhead lights blinked on. Richard leaned in the doorway, fully dressed and ready to ride. "Wondered when you'd make a run for it."

"Oh, Richard, I'm sorry. My head tells me I should stay and wait for Zach to return, but my gut says he's in trouble and might need some help. The least I can do is cover his back."

"Thought you'd feel that way. I guess it wouldn't do me any good to tell you not to go."

She shook her head, her fingers tightening on the horse's reins. "I have to go."

"You're not going by yourself."

"I don't want to put anyone else in danger."

"Too bad. You're not going by yourself. My horse is ready and waiting out front. You have to put up with me in this crazy midnight rodeo."

"You could be shot at."

"Heck, I get shot at all the time by these darned fool weekend hunters who can't figure out the business end of a gun." Richard chuckled. "Come on. Let's you and me go for a ride in the moonlight. It's a mighty fine night for it."

Jacie choked back her response, afraid her voice would shake with her gratitude. Richard had always told her he appreciated her ability to avoid the feminine hysterics most women were prone to. It was one of the reasons he'd hired her. She was a straight shooter and not at all froufrou.

Her heart a little lighter, Jacie led her gelding out into the barnyard where, sure as he'd said, Richard had his black quarter horse saddled and ready to go.

He had a rifle in his scabbard and an old-fashioned revolver in a holster slung around his hips.

The man could have been a gunslinger in a former life, he looked so natural. They left the ranch compound without speaking and nudged their horses into a gallop as soon as they cleared the last gate.

If all went well, they'd be at the ridge of the canyon in less than an hour. Then Jacie would have to decide what next. She didn't know where the Los Lobos hideout was in the maze of canyon trails. Hell, she'd cross that bridge when she came to it. Right now anywhere closer to the canyon where her sister disappeared and Zach had gone to find her was better than waiting around her cabin with someone trying to break in.

ZACH AND JUAN raced back to where the trail led up out of the canyon. As Juan started up the narrow trail, two motorcycles emerged from the shadows Zach had just left. Two more shot out close behind.

Zach turned on his horse and fired at the lead cyclist. His bullet went wide of its target and the cycle continued straight for them.

Four to one wasn't the best odds. Zach could take them, but then he'd waste time. Time was something he couldn't afford to give up. The longer Tracie remained in the clutches of the cartel, the more torture she'd have to endure. And the longer he was in the canyon, the longer he was away from Jacie.

He spun his horse, aimed at the closest pursuer and fired.

The rider jerked off the bike and landed on his back on the ground. The next rider swerved to miss him and slid sideways on the rocky surface. Two down, two more to go. Without cover and concealment, Zach would be at a disadvantage defending himself and if he tried riding up the trail to the top, he might as well paint a target on his back and Juan's. The two pursuers at the bottom only had to dismount and take aim.

Out in the open and out of options, Zach leaped off his horse and slapped the animal's hindquarters, sending it up the hill after Juan.

Zach dropped to the ground, drew his weapon and aimed at the nearest man. When he pulled the trigger, nothing happened.

The men on the motorcycles drew steadily closer.

Zach pulled the bolt back and ejected the bullet inside, then slid it home, aimed and pulled the trigger again.

Nothing.

On the ground, his gun jammed, Zach lay still, hoping to surprise the two men with the only other weapon he had on him. Juan's switchblade.

Chapter Eleven

Jacie and Richard neared the ridge at a trot, glad for the full moon and the near-daylight conditions in which to maneuver the Texas landscape.

The closer she got to the canyon, the faster Jacie's heart beat. She sensed trouble. A nudge to her gelding's flanks urged the animal into a gallop.

Almost at the edge, her horse ground to a halt and reared, his whinny filling the sky. Up over the top of the ridge sprang another horse and rider, charging straight for them.

The horse and rider skirted Jacie but didn't make it past her boss. Richard headed him off, leaned over and snatched the reins out of his hands, jerking the horse to a stop.

A string of Spanish curse words rolled out of the rider's mouth, and Jacie recognized him as Juan, the man who'd been with Zach when they'd taken off on their reconnaissance mission.

Jacie calmed her gelding and joined Richard and Juan.

"Where's Zach?" she demanded.

"I don't know. He was behind me."

The sound of engines carried up to her from the canyon below.

A feeling of déjà vu washed over Jacie and she whirled her mount, heading for the canyon. Before she reached the edge, another horse topped the trail and headed her way. This one was riderless.

Damn. Damn. Damn. Jacie sank her heels into the gelding's flanks, sending him hurtling over the edge and down the trail. Below on the floor of the canyon, two motorcycles were nearly at the base of the path leading upward.

Zach was nowhere to be seen.

Then a shadow sprang up from the ground beside the first motorcycle and the rider was yanked off his seat, landing flat on his back.

The trailing bike veered straight for the two figures grappling on the ground.

Jacie pulled her rifle from the scabbard and, one-handed, fired off a round above the head of the attacker. It didn't deter him a bit. Either he couldn't hear over the roar of the motorcycle engine or he wasn't fazed by gunfire.

Now that the second motorcycle was practically on top of the tangled shadows of the men on the ground, Jacie didn't dare shoot at him for fear of missing and hitting Zach instead.

The rider leaped off his bike and joined the fight.

Jacie let her horse pick his way down the treacherous trail, while her heart hammered against her ribs. She prayed she wouldn't be too late to help.

A shot rang out from below.

Jacie's gelding sidestepped, nearly taking them both over the edge.

One of the shadows fell, lying motionless on the ground. The other two continued the struggle. One of them had to be Zach.

Jacie reached the bottom and charged toward the dueling pair, leaping out of the saddle before the horse came to a complete stop. Still holding her rifle, she pointed it at the pair.

Zach knocked the man to the ground and staggered back, bleeding from a gash on his cheek. The man on the ground rolled to the side, grabbed his fallen weapon and rolled to his back, aiming at Zach.

Jacie fired off a round, hitting the man square in the chest before he had a chance to pull the trigger. His gun fell to the side, and he lay still, his eyes open, staring up at the full moon.

Zach dropped to his knees, breathing hard. "I thought I told you not to come," he grumbled.

"And if I hadn't, you might be dead." Jacie laid

her rifle on the ground and knelt beside him. "Are you okay?" She studied the gash on his cheek and searched him for other signs of injury, wishing she had a flashlight to work with.

"I'm okay." His lips twisted, then straightened into a smile and he shook his head. "Thanks."

"Now, was that so hard?" She pulled his arm over her shoulder and helped him to his feet.

"I'm really okay, just winded."

"Shut up and let me help." She led him to her horse. "Take the saddle. I'll ride behind."

Zach dragged himself up into the saddle.

Jacie assisted with a firm hand on his rear, shoving him upward. She couldn't help thinking that he had a nice behind. Some kind of thought to have when she'd just killed a man.

Holy crap. She'd just killed a man.

Her knees wobbled. The finality of her actions hit her, and her heart nearly stopped.

Zach moved his foot out of the stirrup and reached down for her hand. "Come on. We have to get to Hank's place."

Jacie didn't have time to go soft on him. So she'd killed a man. A man who would have killed Zach if she hadn't. And her sister was still missing.

She straightened her shoulders, dragged in a steadying breath and put her hand in Zach's, her foot in the stirrup.

As he pulled her up, she swung her leg over the horse's hindquarters and landed neatly behind the saddle and Zach, wrapping her arms around his waist.

Zach reined the gelding around and sent it up the trail at a slow, steady pace, letting the horse choose his steps, given that it was carrying double the burden.

Jacie leaned into Zach's back and inhaled the heady scent of dust, denim and cowboy, letting his strength and courage seep into her. She didn't look down, just closed her eyes and let the horse and the man get her out of the hell she'd just experienced.

Richard waited at the top of the hill with the reins of Juan's horse tied to his saddle horn. "I would have come down, but you had it all under control before I could. I take it we need to report a couple of deaths?"

"We'll hit the ops tent on the Raging Bull and let them handle things." Zach glanced around. "Have you seen my horse?"

"He's halfway back to the barn by now."

Jacie couldn't be sorry about that. It meant she didn't have to drive. It gave her an excuse to hold on to Zach a little longer without revealing how needy she actually felt. What was it about this man that made her want to be strong for him at the same time he turned her knees to jelly?

Richard rode ahead with Juan.

Zach and Jacie allowed the gelding to take his time. Moonlight streamed over them and they were alone in the stark Texas landscape.

After a few minutes, Jacie swallowed her disappointment and bucked up the courage to confirm, "I take it you didn't find Tracie?"

"No." The word was terse, almost angry.

"What did you find?"

"Juan was correct in that Los Lobos had a rendezvous point in a cave in the canyon, but they were in the process of relocating because of all the activity in the canyon with the FBI and DEA looking for Tracie and the people who killed their agents."

"Did you find out where they moved Tracie?"

Zach shook his head, staring straight ahead. "Every man I questioned said the same thing. Los Lobos didn't kidnap anyone and they didn't kill the two La Familia Diablos men."

"If not Los Lobos, who?"

"They think that whoever killed the men wanted it to look like Los Lobos to throw the FBI and DEA off the trail of the real killers and to stir up trouble for Los Lobos with La Familia Diablos."

Jacie leaned her forehead into Zach's back. "Then we're back to square one. We don't have a lead and we don't know who took Tracie or where."

His hand rested over hers, warm and gentle. "We'll find her."

"Are you thinking it's someone internal to the FBI or DEA who set this all up?"

"I can't be certain, but I'd bet it is."

"Where do we go next?"

"I'm not sure. First, I need to talk to Hank and an old buddy of mine I trust from the FBI."

"No. First we need to have your wounds tended." Her arms tightened around his middle for a second before she realized he might have been hit in the ribs. She loosened her hold.

"I'm fine. I just need a shower. I can get that back at the Big Elk and you can get some rest."

They rode into the Raging Bull compound and were immediately surrounded by the agents and local law enforcement personnel manning the night shift.

Richard and the groggy ranch foreman took their horses. Richard would borrow one of the Raging Bull trailers to get the horses and himself back to the Big Elk.

After reporting on the two dead men and filling them in on what Zach had discovered, Jacie was so tired she could barely stand.

"Out and about again?" Bruce appeared at Jacie's side. "I thought you'd given up and gone back to the Big Elk." Her sister's boyfriend stood close behind her, his breath stirring the stray hairs resting against her neck.

"Couldn't sleep." Jacie took a step away from Bruce, tucking the loose strands of hair behind her ear and praying Zach would wrap up what he was doing. She was too tired to talk with anyone, especially Bruce.

"Your sister always pushes her hair behind her ear like that."

"What has the FBI come up with so far?" Jacie changed the subject, her gaze still on Zach, willing him to look up.

Several feet away, his head tilted toward the sheriff who'd been giving him the lowdown on retrieval of the two bodies in the canyon, Zach glanced across at her and frowned.

"Not as much as I'd hoped. Whoever took Tracie didn't leave much of a trail."

"At least we can rule out Los Lobos. And if it wasn't Los Lobos, either La Familia has some inside traitors or someone else took my sister. Any guesses?" Jacie finally pinned Bruce with her gaze, her eyebrows rising up her forehead.

Bruce shook his head, his eyes shadowed. "You are a lot like your sister. Get down to the business at hand. That's what I love about her."

"Where is she, Bruce?" Anger fueled by frustration and exhaustion bubbled up inside her. "You have two federal agencies and the local law enforcement on this rescue effort and what have you found? Nothing."

An arm slipped around her waist. "You ready to go, darlin'?"

Zach's resonant baritone washed over her like a soothing warm wave. The tension that had held her upright for the past hour slowly seeped out of her and left her oddly boneless and ready to collapse. Her chin tipped upward and she gave him the hint of a smile. "Yes. I'm more than ready to go."

Zach pulled her against him and stared across at Bruce. "If you don't mind, I'm going to steal my girl away and get her home to bed."

Heat flared in Jacie's body at Zach's words, the images they generated making her tingle all over. Her nipples hardened into tight little buds rubbing against the lace of her bra.

"Take me home," she whispered, leaning into him, grateful for the added support when her knees turned to jelly.

As he drew her away from Bruce, Jacie whispered, "Did you talk to Hank about our next steps?"

"He called it a night an hour ago. I hate to wake the man when there's nothing more we can do tonight."

"Good point."

"We can do that in the morning. Right now I

need that shower and some shut-eye." He glanced over at the young Hispanic seated on the ground beside a parked vehicle, his head in his hands. "Come on, Juan. We'll take you home."

Juan scrambled to his feet and followed Zach and Jacie.

Jacie was past exhaustion, and the worry about her sister weighed so heavily she wanted to burst out crying. But that wasn't the way she worked. The thought of going back to her cabin and collapsing into bed sounded wonderful.

Except her mattress was still on the floor and someone had tried to break in while she'd been in the shower.

She glanced at Zach. No, she wouldn't put that on him, not after all he'd just been through. Jacie could handle a gun and take care of herself for what remained of the night.

Zach promised the sheriff he'd fill out a police report the next day, then he grabbed Jacie's arm and led her to his truck, Juan following.

Without uttering another word, they left the Raging Bull and headed for Wild Oak Canyon then the Big Elk Ranch.

Zach's ribs hurt and the gash on his cheek stung from where one of Hank's employees had cleaned and applied antiseptic ointment to his wound. He'd passed on a bandage, but now was second-guessing that decision.

"Dude, you're one crazy son of a b—"

"Please." Zach cut him off. "I owe you an apology for dragging you into that. But thanks. At least it ruled out Los Lobos as the people who kidnapped Tracie."

"Can I have my knife back now?" Juan asked over the backseat.

"I might be crazy, but I'm not stupid." Zach chuckled. "I'll give you back your knife when I drop you at your home."

Juan leaned back against the upholstery. "Whoever killed the two from La Familia must have wanted this woman really bad. No one messes with La Familia without retribution. As many as there are, someone will pay soon."

Jacie turned sideways and peered over the back of the seat. "If you know anyone around here associated with La Familia, now would be the time to tell us."

"What? Or you'll shoot me?" Juan shook his head. "*No estoy loco.* If I tell you who, everyone will know it was me. I'd be a marked man."

"Give us a hint?" Jacie begged.

"No." Juan stared at Zach in the mirror. "Your woman can shoot me dead, but it would be better than what La Familia would do to me."

Zach nodded. La Familia was known for its

brutality with public beheadings and hangings. Los Lobos was no better, a fact Zach knew from experience. "Leave him alone. He's done enough."

Jacie settled back in her seat, her lips tight. "What about Tracie?"

"I have a contact that might be able to help. And I'll get Hank on it, as well."

Zach dropped Juan at his trailer and handed him his knife. "We're square now?"

Juan peered through the truck's open window at Jacie. "For what it's worth, I didn't know your sister would be a target. She asked when the next shipment would be handed off. All I did was tell her. She gave me five hundred dollars for that information." He snorted. "I should have asked for a lot more."

Jacie's mouth twisted. "And I shouldn't have let her go on the trail that day."

Zach drove out of the little town of Wild Oak Canyon in silence.

The back of Jacie's head rested against the seat, her profile one of natural, wholesome beauty. Unfettered, unblemished beauty that went deeper than skin. "Do you think Juan really knows someone in La Familia?"

Zach drew his attention away from Jacie's profile and back to the road before answering, "Yes."

"Then why didn't you make him tell us who it was?"

"I've seen what these cartels do to the people they deem traitors or informers. Juan did what we asked of him today. We put him in enough danger just associating with us. Besides, I don't think he's involved in what's going on with your sister."

"If he knows who we can ask…"

"He'd be dead by morning if we moved on his information."

"What about Los Lobos? Won't they be after Juan?"

"Maybe, but they didn't see me with him in the canyon. Not where they would recognize him."

Deep in thought, Zach didn't see the other vehicle until it broadsided his truck, metal slamming into metal, forcing him to swerve and bump through the gravel on the roadside. "Hold on!" He gripped the steering wheel with both hands and fought to get it back up on the road.

Jacie grabbed for the handle beside the door and held on, the seat belt tightening, bracing her against the rough terrain.

Zach veered back up onto the road, only to be hit again. This time the truck careened off the road and down the embankment into the ditch and back up on the other side.

The vehicle on the road slowed and the window slid downward.

"Duck!" Zach cried, hitting the accelerator,

sending the truck back down into the ditch and up onto the road.

At the same time, the dark older-model SUV shot forward, catching Zach's truck bed.

The back end swung around, but Zach corrected and hit the gas again, propelling the truck forward.

The vehicle behind him raced to catch up.

In the rearview mirror, all Zach could see was the dark silhouette of the vehicle whose headlights were blacked out.

Something rose above the top of the vehicle behind him, and dread filled his gut. Zach jerked the steering wheel with one hand as he shoved Jacie's head down with the other.

The back windshield exploded inward with a spray of bullets. One zipped all the way through and smashed into the front glass, sending out a spider web of fissures, making it difficult to see.

Zach couldn't outrun the SUV, and the turn-off to the Big Elk Ranch was still several miles away. "Jacie, you're going to have to return fire."

"Are you kidding?"

"It's that or one of us isn't going to make it to tomorrow, maybe both. Use my rifle."

"I'd rather use mine."

She grabbed her rifle from where it rested on the floorboard, removed her safety belt and turned in the seat, steadying the gun's barrel on the back of the headrest.

"What do you want me to aim at?"

"Start with the shooter on top. Hell, just shoot at the whole damn vehicle. It'll be hard enough to hit anything on these bumpy roads."

She fired once.

The vehicle behind them swerved, then straightened.

The next round caused the man on top to duck inside.

Her third round forced the driver to drop back.

"That's my girl." Zach grinned. "You're pretty good riding shotgun."

Still sitting backward in her seat, Jacie smiled. "Knowing how to handle a weapon comes in handy sometimes, besides on the hunt."

The vehicle behind them dropped back farther until it spun around and headed in the opposite direction.

"Thank God." Jacie turned and settled back down in her seat and took stock of the truck. "I'm sorry your truck took the worst of that. And you kept it so nice and shiny."

Zach could have laughed. "To hell with the truck. You could have been hurt."

She glanced his way, one hand clasping her left shoulder. "Uh, actually…" Jacie moved her hand.

Because Jacie had been wearing a dark shirt,

Zach hadn't noticed the blood until the light from the dash glanced off the liquid.

"Damn. We're going straight to the doctor." He slowed, ready to do a U-turn in the middle of the highway.

"It's only a flesh wound and I have no desire to enter into another game of chicken with the SUV that attacked us back there." She pointed to the road ahead. "I have a first aid kit in my cabin. A little disinfectant and a bandage ought to fix me right up."

Zach's foot hovered over the accelerator. "Are you sure?"

"I've lived on a ranch long enough to know a serious wound from a not-so-serious wound. I just want to go home. Please."

Still not fully convinced, Zach gave in and hit the gas, sending the truck shooting forward. He pulled onto the dusty road into the Big Elk Ranch, anxious to get there and assess the damage himself.

The trailer from the Raging Bull was parked beside the barn, empty. Apparently Richard had arrived earlier, taken care of the horses and called it a night.

If need be, he'd take Jacie to the lodge and call an ambulance if her wound was more than just torn flesh.

After parking in front of Jacie's cabin, Zach leaped down and rounded the truck in a jog.

Jacie had the door open and was stepping down.

He grabbed her around the middle and eased her the rest of the way down to the ground.

For a moment he stared down at her, appreciating that she wasn't crying. She hadn't burst into hysterics at the sight of her own blood, and she was staring back up at him, the moon reflected in her eyes.

"Anyone ever tell you that you're an amazing woman?" Zach said.

"No, but you can say it again. It sounds nice." She smiled, and then grimaced. "I'd better get this cleaned up. And you need a bandage on your face."

"We're a pair. We look like we lost the fight."

"The hell we did. We've only just begun." She led the way up the steps to her cabin and fumbled in her pocket for the key.

Before she could find it, Zach pushed the door and it swung open. "Did you lock this door?"

Jacie frowned. "Yes, I did."

When he moved to enter, Jacie held out a hand to stop him.

"Wait," she whispered. "What if someone's inside?"

Zach pulled her to the side and lifted the rifle to his shoulder. "Stay here." He gave her a steady, stern look.

She nodded.

Zach stood to one side of the door, edged it open wider with the barrel of the rifle and peered inside.

Furniture had been upended and papers and clothes scattered across the floor. "I think whoever did this is gone," he said, his voice so low only Jacie would be able to hear him.

Ducking low, he entered the cabin, keeping out of the moonlight streaming through the windows. He worked his way around the cramped interior, checking in the bathroom and closet before he was satisfied that it was no longer occupied.

"It's clear," he called out.

Jacie came inside, closed the door behind her and flipped on the light. The tears welling in her eyes, which she'd refuse to let fall, were Zach's undoing.

He crossed the room and opened his arms. Jacie fell into them, wrapping hers around his waist. "I'm just too tired to deal with this."

"Then don't. All we need is that first aid kit, and we're out of here."

"It was in the bathroom." She leaned away from him and he slipped into the bathroom. "And we don't have to leave. I'm okay."

He stayed in the bathroom longer than necessary to retrieve the kit under normal circumstances.

"Find it?" Jacie asked.

"Most of it." Zach emerged with the kit, stuffing bandages and tubes of ointment into the plastic container. "I have enough to work with." He glanced around the bedroom. "Was your sister staying with you?"

"Yes."

"Did she leave anything here that might explain why she came? Maybe something that would be worth ransacking this place for?"

"I went through her suitcase and discovered her cell phone and FBI credentials. I hid them before I left to find you."

Zach frowned. "Why did you hide them?"

Jacie looked away. "Someone tried to get into the cabin while I was in the bath."

Zach blew out a long breath. "Not good news."

"You're telling me." She stared at the mattress, recalling the cold chill of dread she'd had as she sat on the floor, her gun trained on the door.

"Where did you hide the cell phone and credentials?"

Jacie's lips quirked upward. "In the fridge beneath the rotting bag of tomatoes."

Zach's mouth quirked. "Smart move. Let's hope the intruder didn't figure it out." He picked his way across the floor to the refrigerator, pulled it open and rummaged around inside. He came out with the cell phone, credentials and a tight smile. "You could have been an agent, Jacie Kosart."

She shrugged and grimaced. "Not my calling."

"Come on, we're going to my cabin. Hopefully it's still intact. We can figure out the rest of this mess in the morning." Zach shoved Tracie's phone and wallet inside his back pocket.

"Come closer to the door. I'm going to turn out the lights."

Jacie stood against the wall beside the door, aware of Zach's warmth next to her.

Zach switched the overhead light off, plunging them into darkness. "I'm going out first," he whispered against her cheek.

The warm draft of his breath made gooseflesh rise on her arms. He was close enough to kiss.

"Wait until I tell you to come." He touched her hand and then slipped out the door into the night.

Jacie's heart fluttered and she held her breath for what felt like a very long time. Then the door nudged open.

"It's okay, my cabin's untouched." Zach was there again. He captured her hand in his and led her across to his cabin.

Once inside, Zach closed the shades and pulled the curtains over the windows. Then he switched on the light. "Now let's take care of that wound."

"Earlier…" Jacie stiffened when Zach's fingers reached for the buttons on her blouse. "I can do it." Jacie wasn't sure she could resist him at such close quarters. He drew her like a fly to honey and she was too tired to resist.

He shook his head, his lips firm. "Let me do this. I'm trained in first aid and buddy care."

"My mother taught me enough that I haven't died yet," she argued halfheartedly. Her arm stung and she didn't have the strength to argue. Jacie sighed. "Fine."

He sat on the edge of the bed.

Jacie drew in a deep breath. This was not a good idea. Not when her defenses were down.

Zach stood in front of her and reached for the top button on her shirt. He pushed the button through the hole, then the others, all the way down to where the shirt disappeared into the waistband of her jeans. He tugged the tails free and slid the blouse over her shoulders, easing the fabric over her injured arm.

A quiver of awareness rippled across her skin, and her breasts tightened. Jacie closed her eyes and sucked in a long, steadying breath.

Footsteps sounded, leading into the bathroom. Water ran in the sink and the footsteps returned.

Every one of her senses lit up. With her eyes still closed, she inhaled the scent of Zach, letting it wash away the fear of seeing him fighting two men at once, not being able to help for fear of shooting the wrong man. The way he'd held her the night before, the way she hoped he'd hold her again.

"I'll try to be gentle."

"Just do it," she whispered, praying he would.

Chapter Twelve

Zach was in over his head on this one, with no way to swim to the top.

Jacie sat with her eyes closed, her hair spilling down her back, the light shining down over her face, neck and breasts, giving her a golden glow.

God, she was beautiful.

His hand shook as he smoothed the damp cloth over her wound.

He would never have suspected her skin would be so soft and silky beneath her tough-gal exterior. She smelled like the Texas wind and herbal shampoo as she sat with her eyes closed, her head tilted back slightly, her breathing shallow, the rise of her chest captivating.

Tempted to steal a kiss from those full, luscious lips, he dragged his focus back to the task at hand, shifting uncomfortably as his groin tightened.

After cleaning the wound, he opened the tube of antiseptic, hoping it would bring him back to his senses with its acrid scent. It didn't.

He applied the cream, his gaze slipping to the swells of her breasts, peeking out from the top of a lacy black bra. Who'd have thought the hunting guide would have such a sexy piece of lingerie in her wardrobe? His thoughts shifted farther south. Did she wear matching panties?

Zach fought the urge to slip the strap over her shoulder and bare one of those delicious orbs. He peeled the backing off a large adhesive bandage and taped it to her skin over the injury. "There—" He cleared his throat. "All done."

She turned to him, her eyes opening, the hunger in them hard to miss. "Now your turn," she said, her voice husky and so sexy Zach thought he might lose control.

Holy cow, how was he supposed to sit while she administered first aid to him? He could barely move, he was so hard.

She rose from the bed and walked toward the bathroom, wearing her bra and her jeans, her hips swaying with every step. Perhaps she'd be appalled at how sexy she looked.

Not Zach. He couldn't tear his gaze away from her rounded bottom. A groan rose up his throat.

Jacie was the job. Making love to her wasn't part of the contract. But when she emerged from the bathroom with a damp cloth, all good intentions flew out the window.

She came to a stop in front of him, hesitated a

moment, then straddled his legs and bent down to apply the cloth to the wound on his cheek. Jacie leaned close enough Zach could easily have reached out and touched one of those lace-clad breasts with his lips.

After cleaning the wound, she applied the antiseptic and the bandage, then sighed, straightening. "Am I that homely?" she whispered, then started to step away from him, a frown wrinkling her forehead.

Zach grasped her hips. "What did you say?"

Her cheeks suffused with a pretty pink and she glanced away from him. "Nothing."

"Wrong." He tugged her hips, forcing her to sit on his legs. "Do you know how hard it is to be a gentleman when you're wearing only a bra?" His hands slipped up to the catch at the middle of her back. "When all I want to do is this...." He flicked the hooks open and slipped the straps over her shoulders—gently around her wound. "I just didn't want to cross the line."

She laughed softly, letting the bra fall to the floor. "Don't tell me you're a rule follower. I can't picture you as one."

"Never." He looked up at her, his gaze capturing hers. "You've been through a lot today. Are you sure this is what you want?"

Jacie smoothed a hand over his hair. "I not only want this, I need it." She tugged his ears, dragging him within range of one full, rosy-tipped breast. "Please, don't make me beg."

He couldn't resist the temptation. He sucked her nipple into his mouth, his other hand rising to capture the other breast. His tongue swirled around the tip until it puckered into a tight little bud. He nibbled it and then switched to the other, giving it equal attention.

Jacie's back arched, her bottom squirming against his thighs. They still wore jeans and Zach wanted nothing more than to lie naked beside her and feel all of her against him.

He stood her on her feet and rose from the bed. She frowned. "Is that it?"

"Not unless you want it to be." He shrugged out of his shirt and slung it to the corner.

"No. I want it all." She grasped the top button of his jeans and forced it through the opening. Then she worked the zipper down until his engorged member sprang free.

Zach let out the breath he'd been holding, the relief only temporary. He pulled his wallet from his back pocket, tossed it onto a pillow, then shucked his jeans.

Her gaze followed the path of the descending denim, her tongue sliding across her lips when he stood naked before her. Fire burned through his veins at the hunger in her expression. Past rational thought, he reached for her waistband, ripped the button open and shoved her jeans down her legs until she could kick free of them.

He scooped her up in his arms and laid her across the comforter and then crawled into the bed over her. "We should be sleeping," he said, pressing a kiss to her lips—sleep the furthest thing from his mind.

Her hands laced around his neck, her mouth turning up in a smile. "Sleep is overrated." She pulled him close, capturing his lips, her tongue slipping between his teeth. For every thrust of that magic tongue, an answering tug hit him low in the groin. If he didn't concentrate, it would be over before he had a chance to pleasure her.

He slid his mouth over her chin and down the long line of her throat to the base, where her pulse beat a ragged staccato against her skin. He tapped his tongue to the tip of one breast and captured the other, pulling it fully into his mouth, where he suckled until her back arched off the mattress.

Jacie's fingers wove through his hair and she tugged, urging him lower still. Her thighs parted, allowing him to lie between them on his journey down to her nether regions.

His fingers led the way, parting her folds buried beneath a light smattering of fluffy dark curls. He slid his tongue across the special bundle of nerves packed into a simple nubbin of flesh.

Jacie bucked beneath him, "Oh, Zach!" She

dug her heels into the bed and rose to meet his tongue's every stroke, her fingers digging into his scalp. Her body grew rigid, her thighs tight, her face pinched as she catapulted over the edge.

Zach climbed up her body, rolled to the side and grabbed his wallet from the other pillow, tearing through the contents until his fingers closed around a foil packet. He ripped it open with his teeth.

Jacie pulled the condom free and rolled it down over his swollen member. "Now. Please."

He leveraged himself between her legs and slipped into her warm, wet channel, sliding all the way in. Her muscles contracted around him and he fought for control.

Soon he was thrusting in and out of her, his pace increasing with the intensity of sensations filling his body. The tingling ripped through him from his toes to the tip of his shaft. He rammed home one last time and collapsed on top of her, buried deep inside Jacie's warmth.

Her legs wrapped around his middle, her arms around his neck.

For a long time, he pulsed inside her, the troubles of the world so far away they could have been on an entirely different planet for all he knew.

When his senses finally calmed and he returned to the present, he rolled to his side, taking her with him, their connection unbroken.

She lay with her head pillowed on his arm, her eyelids drifting to half-mast. "Are you always this intense?" She touched a finger to his lip.

He kissed the tip, giving her the hint of a smile. "Only when it counts."

"Um. I'd say it counted." She draped a leg over his, sliding her calf across his thigh.

"To answer your earlier question, no, you're not homely. You're beautiful." He brushed a kiss across her lips and pulled her closer, resting his chin on the top of her head.

Within seconds, Jacie's breathing slowed and her body relaxed against his as she fell asleep.

Zach lay awake for a long time, sanity crowding in on him with each passing minute.

He'd done exactly what he'd sworn he'd never do again. He'd slept with a woman whom he could very easily fall for. Hell, he was already halfway there.

Jacie was everything he could possibly want in a woman. Tall, gorgeous, open, honest and tough enough to set him in his place. She was loyal and loving and deserved a man who could give her all of himself.

Zach just wasn't that man. After what had happened to his partner, he vowed never to become so emotionally committed to any woman. It hurt too badly when you lost her and he knew his heart wouldn't survive another blow that deep.

An hour later, Zach slid his arm from beneath Jacie's neck and climbed out of the bed. He pulled on a pair of jeans, grabbed his cell phone and let himself out of the cabin.

Clouds had moved in to block the moon. Except for the porch lights on the tiny cabins and the security lights on the lodge, everything was shrouded in inky, black darkness.

Zach sat on the porch steps and checked his phone. He'd been so wrapped up in everything that had happened since he'd gone into the canyon to find Los Lobos hideout, then Jacie…he hadn't checked his calls and messages. Only one call had come in. It was from his friend James Coslowski, and he'd left a message.

Zach's heartbeat picked up as he hit the play button.

"Dude, what the hell have you gotten into? Apparently this Kosart woman was working without authority on a case that wasn't assigned to her. The whole bureau is in an uproar and the big bosses are threatening to roll a few heads. Call me when you get this message and I'll fill you in."

Zach dialed James.

"Do you know any other time of the day than middle of the night?" James answered in a whisper. "Let me get somewhere that I won't wake my pregnant wife so I can talk."

A moment later, he spoke in a normal tone. "So you got my message."

"I did. Why is the bureau all up in arms?"

"Classic case of the right hand not knowing what the left hand was doing. DEA supposedly was working the Big Bend area when your Tracie Kosart wandered in and got herself kidnapped and the agents killed. Any luck finding her?"

"None so far."

"It's a shame. I didn't find anything on Tracie. She checks out as a good agent, follows the rules—until now—and keeps her nose clean. Have it on file that she and Agent Bruce Masterson are in a relationship. I'm guessing you already know that since he's been assigned to the team responsible for finding Agent Kosart."

"He's here."

"One of the FBI big dogs, Grant Lehmann, has also assigned himself as overseer of the operation to retrieve the Kosart woman."

"I guess with the two agencies involved, they felt it necessary to have adult supervision?"

"Probably. I found it interesting that one of Bruce Masterson's past assignments was to infiltrate a drug ring in the San Antonio area. He pulled in a pretty major leader on that case and got all kinds of kudos and awards for his work."

"Seems like he needed to be a little farther west."

"Yeah, but the ringleader has connections to people in your area."

Zach sat up straighter. "Names?"

"Let me find my notes." The sound of papers being turned crackled in Zach's ear before James said, "Here it is. The file only listed one, Enrique Sanchez. Lives in a trailer six miles south of Wild Oak Canyon. The notes in the file indicate he makes frequent trips to Mexico and has been seen with members of La Familia Diablos on the Mexican side of the border."

"Anything else?"

"That's all so far. I'll let you know as soon as I dig up anything else."

"Thanks, cos."

"Keep your head down, buddy. It's likely to blow up even bigger than you think. What with two agencies fighting over jurisdiction and blaming each other for everything that's gone wrong."

"Trust me, I'm here. I know." Zach clicked off his cell phone, his heart pumping, sleep so far from his mind he couldn't stay still.

He had to get to Enrique Sanchez. If he was a member of La Familia, he might know what happened to Tracie. Trouble was that he couldn't leave Jacie alone. Not after her cabin had been ransacked. Since whoever had tossed her home had tried to break in while she was there, they weren't concerned about being seen by her. Meaning they would have either taken her or killed her.

Zach would have to wait until Jacie awoke. He'd get the cell phone to Hank's team and let them hack into it for any information they might find. For safekeeping, he'd leave Jacie with Hank and check out Sanchez.

From that point on, Zach spent time cleaning and checking his weapons. He couldn't afford to have one jam on him when he needed it most. And if Sanchez proved to be a member of La Familia, it wouldn't be an easy task to convince him to talk.

SOMETHING BRUSHED JACIE'S lips, tickling her awake in the predawn of morning. She rolled onto her back and blinked open her eyes.

Zach leaned over her, dressed only in jeans and looking so handsome he hurt her eyes.

"Go away," she grumbled, slinging an arm over her face. She probably looked like hell.

"We have work to do. I got a lead."

Jacie sat up straight, forgetting for a moment that she was completely naked. Her face heated and she grabbed the sheet, dragging it up to her chin. "What lead?"

Zach's lips quirked upward, his gaze traveling over her. "The name of a man who could be connected to La Familia."

Jacie flung the sheet back and leaped out of

the bed, all sleepiness forgotten. "Where are my jeans? I need a shirt. Why didn't you wake me earlier? Why are you just standing there?"

He shook his head, unable to hide his smile. "You're beautiful." Zach stepped up to her and finger-combed her hair back off her forehead, his brown eyes darkening to near black.

Jacie's body responded to his light touch. "Not fair. You have all your clothes on."

"I can fix that."

"What about the man from La Familia?"

"It's still dark outside. It can wait until light." Zach wrapped his hands around her waist and pulled her against him, the hardness of his erection pressing into her belly, telling the truth. He wanted her as much as she wanted him.

She circled her arms around his neck and pressed her naked breasts into his chest. "Then what are you waiting for?" Jacie slid her calf up the back of his leg.

Zach kissed her as he cupped her bottom and lifted her, wrapping her legs around his waist and backing her against the wall.

He reached beneath her to unfasten his jeans. His member sprang free and nudged her opening.

"Are you always this hard in the morning?" she asked.

"Always."

She sucked in a deep breath, so ready for him

to come inside her, but not too far gone to be stupid about it. "What about protection?" She kissed his cheek, then his eyelid, trailing her lips across to the other eye.

Zach carried her across to the bed and dumped her on the mattress.

"Hey. That's not very romantic," she protested.

"Shut up and hand me my wallet," he said through gritted teeth.

She found the leather billfold and pulled out a package similar to the one they'd used the night before. "Last one." She waved it at him. "Better make this count."

"Oh, I will." He dove for it.

Jacie dodged him and held it out of his reach. "Not yet."

"What do you mean, not yet?"

"As you eloquently put it, shut up, and let me show you." Her lips curled in a wicked smile. She pressed her palms to his chest, forcing him onto his back. "I hope you're not one of those men who thinks foreplay is overrated."

"I am."

"Then prepare to be proved wrong." She straddled his jean-clad hips, lowering herself enough to touch his hard shaft, but not enough for him to enter her. At the same time, she kissed him full on the mouth, taking his tongue with hers in long, sexy strokes.

Oh, yeah, she liked touching him and could see herself doing it a lot more. If he'd let her.

"Hell, Jacie, I'm about to explode. Could you hurry it up?"

Her lips slid across his chin and down to his chest, where she nibbled on the tight little brown nipples. Jacie wasn't a virgin, but she'd never played with a man before Zach. She liked it a lot. Her trail led her lower, bumping over the taut ripples of the muscles of his abdomen to the thatch of curls at the base of his shaft.

She wrapped her fingers around his hard, thick member. "Is this fast enough?"

"Hell, no." He leaned up on his elbows, his eyes widening as Jacie touched her lips to the tip and swirled her tongue around the circumference.

Zach dropped to his back and sucked in a deep gulp of air. "Wow."

"Like that?" She did it again, this time followed by slipping his shaft into her mouth and applying a little suction.

He groaned, his hands lacing through her hair. "I can't take much more."

She gave it to him anyway, going down on him until he filled her mouth.

Her blood sang, the fire burning low in her belly flaring, crying out for her to get on with it and take him inside her. Now.

Unable to hold out any longer, Jacie sat up,

rolled the condom down over him and mounted, easing down over him.

Zach wrapped his hands around her hips and guided her up and down. "That's nice." Then he flipped her onto her back and thrust into her. "But this is better."

Jacie had to agree as he rocked in and out, the friction sending her to the edge and over.

At the same time as her body exploded in a tingling burst of sensations, Zach hit home one more time and remained buried deep inside.

Minutes later, they both drifted back to earth and the reality of the sunshine edging around the side of the curtains.

Zach rolled to the side, slapped her bottom and smiled. "Get up. We have work to do."

"How can you move after that?" Her body still vibrating with her release, she lay for a moment longer, basking in the afterglow. She moaned and sat up. Today they had to find her sister. "I'll be ready in five minutes." And she dashed for the bathroom.

Inside she stared at the stranger in the mirror. Her face was flushed, her lips bruised, her hair all over the place. Jacie had never felt more alive and desirable than she did at that moment.

She found a plastic-wrapped toothbrush beneath the sink, scrubbed her teeth and finger combed her hair. With nothing to tie it back with, she was forced to leave it down. Then she splashed her face with water and was finally ready to dress. That's when she remembered all her clothes were in the other room and she'd have to parade once more in her birthday suit in front of Zach.

So much for modesty. But then they'd made love twice. Why should it matter? With a deep breath, she threw back her shoulders and marched out.

Zach held her jeans and one of his T-shirts. "Yours was torn and bloody."

When she held out her hand for them, he raised them out of reach, his gaze panning her body from top to toe. "If only we had more time."

His heated gaze made her body burn. "If only my sister wasn't still missing." She wiggled her fingers, wishing she had the luxury of lying around in bed with Zach all day. "Your T-shirt will fit me like a dress."

"It'll look better on you than it does on me." Zach handed over the clothes, his fingers dropping to tweak her naked breast before he sighed and stepped away. "I called Hank. He's expecting us in thirty minutes."

"Then we'd better get going." She slipped her arms into his T-shirt and pulled it over her body.

Zach's gaze followed the fabric all the way down.

"Eyes up here, cowboy." Jacie pointed to her own eyes and laughed.

"Can't help it. You have a great body."

Her cheeks heated again. "Let's find my sister and you can tell me more about it." Jacie pulled her jeans up over her legs and zipped them, deciding going commando wasn't so bad after all. Once she had her boots on, she glanced around the room. "You have my sister's phone?"

Zach patted his pocket. "I do."

"Then let's go."

At the door Zach pulled her back and into his arms. "You know I leave after this job is over."

Jacie swallowed hard, pasting a smile on her face. "I know. I'm just in this for the sex," she shot back at him as flippant as she could make it sound.

Then she pushed through the door, her chin held high, her heart sitting like a lead weight in her belly. Hell, she'd known from the start that Zach was on assignment from Hank's talent pool. He'd move on to the next job once they found Tracie. Jacie had known the ending of their story from the start, and she'd chosen to have sex with Zach anyway.

Still, the thought of Zach leaving made her day duller and darker than the rain-laden skies. Finding her sister would be bittersweet, but it had to happen.

Chapter Thirteen

Zach dropped the cell phone on Hank's desk. "Can you have someone hack into this and see if there are any numbers or information Tracie might have been using to go after the DEA agents?"

"Will do. My tech guy, Brandon Pendley, just got in and I had him working on hacking into the FBI database." Hank stood with the phone in his hand. "I'm sure this will be a piece of cake for him."

"While you're with Pendley, I need information on Enrique Sanchez. Anything you can find out. His address, family, friends. Anything. As soon as you can get it."

Hank's gaze moved from Zach to Jacie. "Someone we should be aware of?"

"I got word that he's connected with La Familia. Jacie and I will hit the diner and see if we can find out anything else about him. Then I'm going to pay him a little visit."

"I'll get Pendley right on it." Hank frowned. "If

you think you need backup, I can have three other CCI men in less than an hour—including me."

Zach nodded. "I'll let you know. Have Pendley call or text the information as soon as he has anything."

"Will do." Hank nodded toward the window. "The joint operations team is expanding their search, supposedly sending feelers out to the other side of the border to see if they can locate Tracie. The FBI regional director is an old friend of mine, Grant Lehmann. He said he was giving the search top priority."

Jacie inhaled and closed her eyes for a moment. "It just seems so pointless. Is anyone actually going to find her?"

Zach slipped an arm around her and hugged her close. "Yes. And we're going to start by following the leads to Enrique."

"Let me get Brandon on this phone and the information you need to find Enrique. Then before you go, let me arm you with a few things you might need in your efforts. I should have given them to you before, but I wasn't sure if you'd actually employ them." Hank waved them to the back of the house and down the steps to a reinforced basement.

The first room they entered had computer screens lining the desks and larger screens affixed to the walls.

A young man wearing blue jeans, his hair hanging down to his collar and a single earring on one ear, glanced up. "Hey, Hank, who've you got with you?"

"Brandon, meet Zach Adams and Jacie Kosart."

Brandon stood and held out his hand to Jacie. "You're the twin?"

Jacie shook his hand. "That's right. I'm Tracie Kosart's sibling."

"Sorry about your sister."

"Don't be, just help me find her."

"On it." Brandon shook hands with Zach. "Nice to finally meet you in person."

"Actually," Hank added, "it was Brandon that found you and recommended I hire you."

Zach grinned. "Thanks. I think."

"Hank's a good man. You'll like working with him."

Zach made note of the fact that Brandon had said working with Hank, not for him. That indicated a level of teamwork and trust, reinforcing Zach's decision to go to work for Hank.

Hank handed the cell phone to Brandon. "Tracie Kosart's cell. Hack it for any information you can get out of it. But before you start, locate Enrique Sanchez for us."

Brandon gave a mock salute. "On it." He dropped back into his chair, and his fingers flew over the keyboard, his concentration fully on the screen in front of him.

"Brandon will have information about Enrique before you leave the ranch." Hank swept his hand to the back of the room. "Now, if you'll follow me."

Zach wondered how large the basement actually was as he followed Hank deeper into the maze.

Hank stopped at a steel, reinforced door and clicked numbers into a keypad. The door slid open and he stepped aside and gestured for them to follow. "Please."

Inside, the walls were painted a stark white and lined with racks filled with every kind of weapon imaginable.

Jacie spun in a circle, her eyes wide. "Holy crap, Hank, where'd you get all these?"

"Some of them I bought, others I had manufactured in one of my plants." He pulled a canvas bag off a hanger and handed it to Zach. One by one, he plucked armament off the shelves. "You might be able to use these incendiary grenades if you need to create a diversion." He tucked the grenade into the canvas bag and moved to the next shelf labeled CS Gas. "If you need to get the enemy out of a reinforced location, these come in handy. Here, you might need these, as well." Hank handed him a pair of night-vision goggles.

"Hank." Zach shook his head. "I'd be scared if I wasn't convinced you were one of the good guys."

"I wanted my operatives to be prepared for any event."

Zach held up his hand as Hank prepared to shove more into the canvas bag. "I'd never get past the gauntlet of the joint ops team outside with much more than I have in here now. I could use nine-millimeter ammo and a couple tracking devices."

"Got it." Hank handed Zach several clips and boxes of rounds and a web belt with straps that would hold clips and grenades. "And take this." He handed him a shiny SIG Sauer Pro. "In case you need a backup."

Zach stuffed it all into the canvas bag. "That should about cover a small war."

"You're in cartel territory," Hank reminded him. "They have far more firepower than that." The older man handed him three small disks. "Keep one somewhere on your person at all times. Tuck it in your underwear or shoes, just don't let it out of your reach. If you get into trouble, I'll be able to locate you."

"Sounds like you expect big trouble." Jacie shivered.

Zach wished he could shield her from all this, but she was smack dab in the middle and might as well be mentally as well as physically prepared with major hardware. "When we locate your sister, she's likely being held in a guarded compound. Getting in might not be a problem. Getting out with your sister will prove more challenging."

Jacie's chin tipped upward, though her face had paled several shades. "I'm not afraid."

Hank stared hard at her. "You should be. The cartels are ruthless."

Zach nodded. "He's right. I've seen what they can do to a captured woman. It's not pretty." He closed his eyes as memories of Toni's torture washed over him. "On second thought, Jacie, you should stay here with Hank. You'd be better off here monitoring efforts than getting caught up with the cartel."

"You know how well I stay put. Take me with you now or I'll follow you anyway."

Hank chuckled. "I might have to hire you onto my team. I hear you're a good shot."

Jacie nodded. "I am. But I'm not interested. I like my job. Getting shot at by a negligent hunter isn't nearly as scary as getting shot at by an angry cartel member."

Hank shrugged. "The offer's there if you change your mind."

Zach hooked Jacie's arm. "If you're done negotiating, let's get out and find your sister."

Jacie shook her arm loose as she exited Hank's

armory. "What? You don't like the idea of me playing undercover cowboy?" Her eyes narrowed. "Why?"

"It's too dangerous."

"And it's not as dangerous for you?" She flipped her ponytail over her shoulder. "Sounds a bit chauvinistic to me."

At that moment, they passed Brandon's desk. "Give it up, dude. You'll never win."

Zach growled, his gut in a knot at the thought of Jacie being in harm's way every day. She made a good point about double standards, but he couldn't help it. His instinct to protect her was strong and he was struggling to get past it. If he could tie her up at Hank's and be assured she wouldn't find a way loose, he'd have left her rather than take her with him to interrogate Enrique.

Brandon gave Zach a sticky note. "That's Enrique's home address. It's just outside town. Be careful, the man has a police record of assault and battery. He's a mean dude."

"Thanks." Zach tucked the note in his pocket and placed his hand on the small of Jacie's back, guiding her toward the stairs.

"For the record, take the job if you like. It's your life."

Jacie paused with one foot on the step. "That's

right. It is my life. And you're not staying around anyway, so why should it bother you?"

His gut clenched. He'd told her that he'd be out of there as soon as the case was over. Why it hurt hearing this from her, he didn't know, but it did. Zach had to remind himself not to get attached, although he feared it was too late. "Now that we're agreed, keep moving or we'll be here all day." He slapped her bottom as she climbed the steps out of the basement.

"My, my, we're grumpy, aren't we?" She threw a twisted smile over her shoulder at him. "Didn't get enough sleep?"

Her teasing wink only made him want to spank her again, or kiss her. Either would have been just as satisfying at that point, but not nearly enough. He wanted to take her back to bed and make love to her.

Unfortunately now was not the time or place.

"Here, hold this, it will look less conspicuous than if I walked out carrying it." He handed the canvas bag to Jacie before they left the ranch house and crossed to where he'd parked his truck. He glanced up at the steely gray skies, glad for the added darkness, yet hoping the rain would hold off until he had a chat with Enrique.

Bruce Masterson emerged from the operations tent and waved at them. "Jacie!"

"Just keep going," Zach urged.

Jacie placed a hand on Zach's arm and brought him to a stop. "What if he has information about Tracie?"

Zach smiled down at her and spoke between clenched teeth. "You're carrying weapons that aren't necessarily legal for civilians to own."

"Oh." Jacie hiked the bag higher on her shoulder. "Now's a good time to tell me."

"Just make it short." Zach turned to face the FBI agent and nodded, his arm slipping around Jacie, pressing her and the bag against his side. "Masterson."

"Adams." Bruce nodded curtly toward Zach and turned his attention to Jacie. "We got a possible lead on your sister's location."

Jacie's eyes widened and she started to take a step forward.

Zach held her firmly in place, schooling his face to give away nothing. If the FBI truly had a lead, good. In the meantime, they had their own information to follow up on. But he'd hear the agent out.

"Where is she?" Jacie asked. "Is she okay?"

Bruce raised his hand and snorted. "Not so fast. It's a lead, not yet confirmed. I sent agents across the border to check it out. I'll let you know as soon as I find out anything."

"Oh, thank you." She touched Masterson's arm.

"Where will you be? Do you have a number I can reach you at?"

Jacie hesitated.

"You can leave word at the Big Elk Lodge," Zach offered. "Giddings will pass the message on."

"Right." Jacie gave the man a stiff smile. "I'll be busy working outside, away from my phone and out of decent reception."

"Okay, then." Bruce clapped his hands together. "I feel good about this, so don't go too far out of touch in case we bring her back. I'm sure Tracie will want to see you."

Jacie sighed. "Just bring her back alive."

"We will." Bruce spun on his heel and returned to the tent.

Zach turned Jacie toward his truck.

"Why did you tell him to call the lodge?" Jacie asked. "I'll have my phone on me."

"I'd just as soon not give him the number. You don't know who in that operations tent is on our side. Remember there's a mole inside either the FBI or the DEA. We're not sure which, but I'm not willing to take chances."

"Right." Jacie nodded. "And phones can be traced through the global positioning system."

Zach handed her up into the truck and closed the door before climbing into the driver's seat.

They accomplished the drive to town in silence.

As soon as they headed back out of town on the other end, Zach's fingers tightened on the wheel. "I'm not going to drive right up into Enrique's yard."

Jacie turned toward him. "I'm listening."

"I'll park the truck back about half a mile from his place, hide it in the brush and hike in on foot. I'm going to pretend I broke down. That way they don't start shooting right away."

"Sounds good so far."

He breathed in and let it out, then continued, knowing exactly what her reaction would be to his next words. "I want you to stay with the truck and watch for other vehicles that might enter or leave."

"In other words, you're not taking me in." She crossed her arms. "You know how I feel about that."

"I need live backup. By staying back, if you hear gunfire, get the hell back to town, where you'll have cell phone reception and can get Hank's help."

She shook her head. "Not getting any better. Why can't I come with you and we pretend we're the happy, lost couple?"

"Because Enrique might know you or recognize your face if he had anything to do with Tracie's disappearance. It would be like waving a red flag in the bull's face."

Jacie sat back against her seat, her gaze riveted

on his. Finally she sighed, her shoulders sagging. "I hate it when you make sense. Okay, I'll stay put, but I'm not going to like it."

"Thanks." He pulled off the highway and onto the side of the road, bumping across the uneven terrain, fitting the truck in the middle of a clump of scrubby juniper trees.

Cedar scent filled the interior of the truck.

Zach switched the engine off and faced Jacie. "I also didn't want to worry about you." He leaned across the seat, cupped the back of her neck and kissed her soundly on the lips. "Damn it, you're growing on me and it scares the crap out of me."

A lump formed in Jacie's throat. "Goes the same for me."

Zach climbed out of the truck and struck out across the scrubby terrain without a backward glance.

The sky rumbled in the distance, and a single raindrop hit the windshield. Jacie hoped the rain would hold off a little longer until Zach came back.

ZACH RAN PARALLEL to the highway until he reached the dirt track leading into Enrique's place. Old cars littered the front yard, some with the hoods lifted, others jacked up, the tires long gone.

Though he knew he'd be a big target, Zach

stepped out in the open, pretending to be a motorist whose car had broken down on the highway.

"Hello. Anyone home?" Zach called out. No one answered.

The flutter of a curtain in a window of the house caught his attention. A woman's face appeared, then disappeared.

A child cried inside and was quickly hushed.

"Hello." Zach walked closer. "My truck broke down. I need to use a telephone."

The front door opened and a short, round, Hispanic woman peered out. She waved her hands as if to shoo him away, speaking in rapid-fire Spanish, almost too fast for Zach to understand.

He caught the gist of what she was saying, something about leaving before her husband returned.

"I'm sorry." Zach held his hands palms up. "I don't speak Spanish. Do you speak English?"

"No," the woman said.

"She doesn't, but I do." A man appeared around the side of the house, carrying an semiautomatic rifle. "What do you want?"

"My truck broke down on the road and I need to use a telephone."

"We don't have a telephone." He tipped the rifle. "Leave."

"You don't happen to have a tire iron, do you?" Zach moved closer, pretending to be unaffected by the presence of the rifle. "My tire went flat and I can't get the lug nuts loose."

"You can't stay here. Leave now." The man pointed the rifle at him.

"Hey, it's okay." Zach raised his hands. "I just need a tire iron with a lug wrench on it and I'll be out of your hair." He walked around the side of the house.

The man Zach suspected was Enrique followed. "You can't stay."

Once he'd rounded to the back, Zach noted a truck standing with doors wide open. Boxes and furniture had been thrown into the bed as if in a hurry. "Going somewhere, Enrique?"

Zach spun and lunged for the rifle before the man had a chance to fire. He grabbed the barrel, jammed the nose down and the butt up, hitting the guy in the face, causing his hands to loosen enough that Zach ripped the weapon out of his hands and flung it to the side. He yanked the man's arm around to his back and drove it up between his shoulder blades. "Enrique Sanchez, I understand you're a member of La Familia."

"I don't know what you're talking about." He stood on his toes, his face creased in pain.

"Really?" Zach twisted the arm tighter until the man cried out. "Wanna rethink that response?"

"Sí, sí," Enrique squeaked. "I am. So? What do you want?"

"Answers." The clock was ticking on Tracie's life, and Zach had let it go on for too long.

"I don't know anything," Enrique insisted.

"Were you there when the DEA agents were murdered in Wild Horse Canyon?" Zach bore upward on the arm.

"Sí, sí. Madre de Dios!"

"Who murdered the DEA agents?"

Enrique didn't answer.

Zach hated doing it, but he ratcheted the man's arm tighter. "Who killed the DEA agents?"

"Áya! Go ahead, break it! Nothing you can do to me will be as bad as what La Familia will do if they get to me first. So go ahead. Kill me. I am a dead man already."

"Why?"

"I was supposed to meet *mi compadres,* but when I got there, they were dead. La Familia will blame me."

"Did you see who killed them?" Zach loosened his hold, finally letting go.

"No." Enrique dropped to his knees. "I don't know."

"Did you see who took the woman?"

"No." Enrique struggled to his feet. "I have to leave. I have to get my family out before—"

"Zach, look out!"

A shot rang out and Enrique jerked forward,

slamming into Zach, his eyes wide, blood oozing from the wound in his gut.

Zach staggered backward as Enrique slid to the ground, his eyes wide and vacant. The man was dead.

Chapter Fourteen

Jacie sat for as long as she could stand before she flung the door open and dropped down out of the truck. Zach had been gone too long, as far as she was concerned. He could be in trouble.

She grabbed her rifle and tucked her nine-millimeter in her waistband, then set off in the same direction as Zach had minutes earlier. Staying low, she used the available vegetation for concealment as she'd seen Zach do, moving parallel with the highway. When she came to the dirt track leading into Enrique's place, she stopped and listened, then turned and worked her way slowly toward the house.

Nothing stirred out front, so she circled wide, around the back of the house and the workshop behind it.

Voices carried to her, urgent and angry.

One belonged to Zach.

Her heartbeat fluttered and her palms sweat as she eased around the back of the workshop to get a better view, her rifle in front of her, in the ready position.

Zach stood with his back to her.

A man, who Jacie assumed was Enrique, was on his knees in front of Zach, struggling to stand. With only the one man in sight, Jacie gathered that Zach had everything under control. She had started to back away when she saw a movement from the corner of the house.

The barrel of a military-style rifle poked out.

"Zach, look out!" she yelled.

A shot rang out. Enrique, who'd managed to stand, dropped to the ground.

As a man stepped away from the side of the house, Jacie crouched to a kneeling position, aimed for the man's chest and pulled the trigger.

The shooter dropped to the ground before he could fire off another round.

Jacie's pulse pounded so hard the blood thrummed against her eardrums. She didn't hear the footsteps behind her until too late. A rock skittered by her, her first indication she was not alone.

Jacie rolled to her back, holding her rifle to her chest. Before she could aim and fire, a boot punted the rifle out of her hands.

A bulky, dark-haired, barrel-chested man grabbed the front of her shirt and yanked her to her feet.

Jacie kicked and fought to get free.

The bulk of a man spun her around like a rag doll, pinned her arms behind her and pulled the pistol from her waistband, tossing it to the side. He shoved her forward into the clearing.

Zach crouched, holding his weapon in front of him. When he spotted Jacie, his eyes widened. "Jacie."

"I'm sorry," Jacie said. "I thought you were in trouble."

"Drop the gun," the man holding Jacie demanded in a heavy accent.

"Don't hurt her." Zach tossed his pistol to the ground and raised his hands.

Another man came running around the side of the house, cursing as he leaped over the body of his dead *compadre*. He ran straight up to Zach and hit him hard with the butt of his high-powered rifle.

Zach dropped to the ground and didn't move.

Jacie cried out and lunged forward.

Meaty hands squeezed her arms so hard that pain shot up into her shoulders.

The two men spoke Spanish so fast Jacie couldn't begin to translate with her own rudimentary skills in the language. By their urgent tone and the way they kept looking over their shoulders, they were anxious to leave.

One of the men ran for the workshop.

Jacie stared at Zach, willing him to get up.

He lay so still, a gash on his forehead where the thug had hit him with the rifle.

Jacie struggled again, fighting past the pain of having her arms pulled back so hard.

Her captor loosened his hold long enough to punch her in the side of the head.

Pain rattled around her head, and fog tinged the edges of her vision.

The other guy emerged from the workshop carrying a roll of duct tape.

Pushing past her fuzzy-headedness, Jacie kicked and bucked, trying to twist loose of the hands holding her like steel clamps. If they got the duct tape around her wrists and ankles, she wouldn't have a chance.

She dug her booted heel into the man's instep and backed into him, ramming her elbow into his gut.

He yelled and hit her again.

Jacie fought the pain, struggling to stay upright and losing. This time, the gray fog won, shutting out the sunshine and dragging Jacie into darkness.

LIGHT EDGED BENEATH Zach's eyelids, and the soft keening wail of a woman crying stirred him to wake. He opened his eyes and winced at the harsh light shining straight into his face from the setting sun. His head ached as he fought to regain his senses.

The crying continued and a baby's whimpers added to the sadness.

Zach turned his head in the direction of the sound, and a bolt of pain shot through his temple, clouding his vision.

A woman knelt in the dirt beside a man's body, a baby clutched to her chest. She rocked back and forth, tears coursing down her cheeks.

Enrique. The cloud over his brain lifted and Zach jerked to a sitting position. He swayed and braced his hands against the earth to keep from falling over.

The woman cried out and scooted away, holding the baby tightly.

Zach raised his hands, then pressed one to his temple where a knot had formed. He winced. "I'm not going to hurt you." He closed his eyes and fought a bout of nausea, then pushed to his feet, his mind coming alive. His first thought was Jacie.

Everything came back to him in a rush. He dug in his pocket for his cell phone and hit the speed dial for Hank. No service.

"Do you have a phone?" he asked the woman on the ground, holding up his cell phone at the same time.

She shook her head, her tears flowing faster.

"Sorry, I can't stick around to help. I'll send someone out." He didn't know if the woman understood what he'd said, but he didn't have time to translate.

He jogged around the house and workshop, his first instinct relief that he hadn't found Jacie's body. His second, dread at what she would be subjected to. He had to get to her before the cartel carried her back across the border and did what they'd done to Toni.

A lead weight settled hard in his gut. He pushed aside the negative thoughts and sprinted back down the road and out to the highway. Once he found his truck, he raced back to town.

As soon as he came close, he checked his service and dialed Hank.

"Zach, where have you been? I've been trying to get in touch with you for the past hour."

"La Familia has Jacie."

"Any idea where they took her?"

"None." That lead weight flipped over in his belly. With no leads, no inkling of where they'd have taken her, he had nothing. Jacie would suffer. "I need you to get Pendley to bring up the tracking devices. If she still has hers on her, we have a chance."

"Pendley hacked into Tracie's phone. Other than Juan Alvarez's number and Bruce Masterson's, there weren't any others leading anywhere."

"And how is that helping me?" Zach drove through town faster than the posted speed limits.

"Pendley checked Bruce Masterson out and found several calls to a Humberto Hernandez at the Big Elk Ranch."

"Isn't he the other guide that works with Jacie?"

"He's the one."

"Did you question Bruce?"

"Haven't seen him in the past three hours. The other agents manning the ops tent said he took off saying he was checking on a lead. I called Richard Giddings and asked him to keep an eye on Humberto until you got there. He called me just a moment ago to say Humberto is saddling a horse and that he'd try to stall him, but he didn't know how without letting on that he's now a person of interest."

"I'll be at the Big Elk in ten minutes. In the meantime, find Jacie's tracker." Zach pressed his foot down hard on the accelerator as his truck headed out of town on the highway leading to the Big Elk Ranch. With Humberto being his only lead, he had to get to him before the guide took off.

The ten minutes might as well have been ten hours. Topping speeds of over one hundred miles an hour, he reached the ranch gate in eight minutes. His truck bed spun around as he turned onto the gravel road to the lodge. Zach straightened the wheels and kicked up a cloud of dust all the way to the lodge. Without stopping, he drove around the big cedar and rock building, skidding to a halt in front of the barn.

Zach grabbed his Glock, dove out of the truck and raced for the barn.

Richard Giddings stood to the side of the door and pointed toward the interior.

With his Glock leading the way, Zach ducked around the door and into the shadows. He paused for a moment to allow his sight to adjust to the limited lighting in the barn's interior.

"I know you're there." Humberto cinched the girth around the gelding he had saddled and dropped the stirrup into place. "Don't try to stop me. I have to make things right."

Zach stepped out of the shadows into the beam of light from an overhead bulb. He pointed his pistol at Humberto's chest. "If you want to make things right, start by telling me where you're going."

"After Masterson."

"Why?"

The man bowed his head for a moment, then raised it and stared at Zach. "I made a mistake."

Zach drew in a frustrated breath. "Could you be a little clearer?"

"I trusted Masterson. He told me I was helping with an undercover operation." Humberto slid a bridle over the horse's nose. "We had a routine. He'd call and let me know when an agent was coming through the Big Elk to pass information on to their undercover operative in La Familia. I got them to the canyon, they passed the information and I made sure they got out of the canyon. Until two days ago."

"What happened two days ago?" Zach stepped closer, his heartbeat kicking up a notch.

"You know what happened. Those DEA agents were murdered and Jacie's sister was taken."

"Why is that your responsibility?"

"Masterson told me to guide different hunters, but they canceled at the last minute. I was supposed to guide the guests going south, but Jacie insisted on taking them. If I'd known they were agents, I would have been prepared for the attack. Instead Jacie and her sister took the hit and the men were killed." Humberto's lips thinned. "I tried to tell myself Masterson had been mistaken. But the more I thought about it, the more I realized Masterson had been using me.

"The men he'd set up to make the drop backed out when they discovered DEA agents were onto them. Afterward I found out Jacie's sister was an FBI agent. That's when I knew something wasn't right." The man's hands shook as he adjusted the straps on the bridle.

Zach's gut told him Humberto was telling the truth. "Where are you going?"

"I asked one of my cousins to snoop around and

find out where La Familia would hole up when things got hot. I know where to start. There's an abandoned ranch house south of here, close to the border. They could be holding Tracie there." He gathered the reins and stepped toward Zach. "I have to make this right."

Zach grabbed the man's arm. "You can't do it alone."

"I feel as responsible for those DEA agents' deaths as if I'd pulled the trigger myself. And if I had been there instead of Jacie and her sister, her sister wouldn't be missing. I have to do this."

"Not without me," Zach said. "I'm going with you."

"I'm going too." Richard Giddings entered the barn.

"No." Humberto raised a hand. "You both need to stay with Jacie and make sure nothing happens to her."

Zach's chest tightened. "It already has."

Humberto closed his eyes and muttered a curse in Spanish.

Richard closed the distance between them. "What's happened to Jacie? Where is she?"

Zach told them what had occurred at Enrique's place and that as far as he could tell, Jacie had been gone nearly three hours. Plenty of time to get far away.

"They wouldn't try to cross the border during

the daylight." Humberto glanced at the barn door where sunlight streamed in, casting long shadows. "It will be dark soon."

Zach's cell phone vibrated in his pocket. He dug it out and noted Hank's number. "Did you find her?"

"Yes, south of here, near the border. I'm not sure what's out there, but we have a GPS coordinate on her. Based on the county map, it's an abandoned ranch house. Do you want me to let the joint operations folks know?"

Zach's fingers tightened around the phone. "Not yet. They might try to fly in with a chopper. There's little enough vegetation to hide a chopper, and they'd hear it long before it got close. Wait two hours and then send them in. That should give us enough time to get down there on horseback and scope out the situation. I don't want La Familia to get spooked and shoot their witnesses." His heart pinched at the thought of what might happen if the cartel got wind that they'd been discovered.

"Us?" Hank asked. "How many of you are headed out?"

"Three." Zach stared at the men beside him, realizing he was going into a tight situation with two men untrained in special operations. But he had to take what he had and get down there. If nothing else, they could shoot and provide cover for him.

"I can have myself and three other men available in the next hour," Hank offered.

"We can't wait. Send the others in only if they can get there before you notify Joint Operations. You'll need to stay and make sure the FBI and DEA launch on time." Zach checked his watch. "It should be dark in one hour. That gives us another hour to get close and locate Tracie and Jacie."

"Godspeed, Zach." Hank ended the call.

"You should take Thunder. He's one of my fastest horses and he's surefooted in the dark." Richard Giddings headed for a stall and lead a black stallion out. "Are you a good rider? This horse can be a bit high-spirited."

"I can handle him." Zach ducked into the tack room and retrieved a saddle and blanket, his pulse hammering, urging him to hurry. The longer it took them to get down there, the more time the cartel had to harm Jacie and her sister.

Richard tied the horse to the stall door and headed for another stall. He led a sorrel gelding out and threw a saddle over his back.

Zach saddled the stallion and slung a bridle over his head. "We'll need saddlebags and scabbards."

Richard nodded to Humberto. "Handle that. I need to duck up to the lodge for a moment."

Humberto retrieved the necessary items, securing the scabbards and saddlebags to the back of Richard's and Zach's horses.

Zach ran out to his truck, gathered the canvas bag, web belt, his rifle and the SIG Sauer Hank had loaned him. He met Richard on the way back to the barn.

The man carried an M110 sniper rifle and had another slung over his shoulder. "Thought we could use some more firepower." His pockets were loaded with boxes of shells and he had two ammo belts looped over his other shoulder. He shrugged. "Our guests like to fire different types of weapons."

Zach smiled grimly. "Glad you cater to them. These will come in handy."

They loaded the magazines, fit the extras into the web belts and tested the weapons. All their preparations took less than fifteen minutes. Fifteen minutes Zach felt they couldn't spare but had to in order to go into cartel-held territory. As the sun sank toward the horizon, the three men mounted and aimed their horses south, setting off at a trot to spare the horses.

Zach prayed they were headed in the right direction and that they wouldn't be too late.

Chapter Fifteen

"Wake up," a man's voice yelled in Jacie's ear.

She wavered in and out of consciousness.

A hard slap to the face jerked Jacie out of the black abyss. She blinked open her eyes. The room around her was dark with one light shining overhead and dust moats floating in and out of its beam.

"Wake up," the deep, intense voice repeated.

Jacie turned to face her nemesis. "What do you want from me?"

"Nothing. It's what I want from her." He pointed to the woman sitting in the shadows, her wrists and feet bound to a chair, her hair drooping in her face.

As the dust moats cleared and Jacie's gaze came into focus, she gasped. "Tracie?"

"Oh, Jacie, I'm so sorry." Her sister's voice cracked. Her face was bruised, her lips split and one eye was swollen shut.

Jacie lunged toward her sister, realizing too

late that her own hands and feet were bound with duct tape to the chair in which she sat. The seat toppled and she landed on her side, her head bouncing off a dirty, splintered wooden floor. It was then she noted the windows had been painted black. Even then, no light shone through or around. It could be dark outside for all she knew. How long had she been out? And what had happened to Zach?

Her heart clenched. God, she prayed the men who'd taken her hadn't shot Zach and left him to die as they had Enrique.

"Don't hurt her," Tracie cried. "She doesn't know anything."

"With her here, maybe you'll start talking." He spoke perfect English with no hint of an accent.

Jacie stared at the man with the voice. He wore a black mask over his eyes, and a black bandana covered his hair like an evil Zorro. "Why are we here? What do you want with us?"

"I want your sister to tell me why she came to Wild Horse Canyon. Who sent her?"

"I told you." Tracie shook her head, wincing as if the effort was painful. "No one sent me. I came on my own."

"Why?"

"To visit my sister."

"Lies!" The man pulled Jacie back up, chair and all, and slapped her face hard.

The blow was hard enough that her teeth rattled and her head swam.

"No, don't!" Tracie cried. "She's just a trail guide. Nothing more."

The man stepped away from Jacie and ran a finger along Tracie's face, brushing across her swollen eyes and lips. "But then you aren't, are you? Who in the FBI sent you down here?"

"No one." She heaved a tired sigh. "It's the truth."

"Then why did you come here?" He moved back to stand beside Jacie, his hand rising. "Tell me now or your sister suffers for you."

"Don't!" Tracie strained against her bonds.

"Your memory returns?" the man asked.

"I came because I read a text on my boyfriend's cell phone. One that asked a man to assist the Big Elk transfer."

"You didn't get orders from your supervisor?"

"No. I was concerned because it was the Big Elk. I wanted to know what it was about since my sister works at the Big Elk Ranch."

"Who did you notify of your search?" he demanded.

"No one."

The hand descended, lashing across Jacie's face

with sufficient force to create a resounding echo in the empty room.

Jacie rocked sideways in her chair, her head reeling. "Leave her alone. She came to see me."

"No, Jacie, I came to find out what Bruce was up to." She stared across at Jacie and sighed. "I had a friend trace the text and it went to Humberto Hernandez."

"The Big Elk's guide?" Jacie closed her eyes and opened them, hoping to regain focus. "How does he know Bruce?"

"I don't know. But I couldn't let it go. I had to know what was going on and what danger you might be in on the Big Elk."

"All very touching. Who else knows of Masterson's contact?"

"No one but you, Bruce and Humberto, as far as I know," Tracie answered.

The man raised his hand to hit Jacie again.

She couldn't help it. Jacie flinched back in her chair.

"Then why did you contact Hank Derringer for assistance?" the man demanded, his hand poised to strike.

Tracie leaned forward, constrained by the bindings. "I wasn't sure what I was up against and when it would go down, so I asked him to help me. Only he didn't have anyone available right away. I didn't tell him why I'd come, just that I might need his help."

"So you came to prove your boyfriend was a traitor?"

"I didn't want to believe it, but I had to know." She slumped in her chair, tears trickling down her cheeks.

Jacie's heart bled for her sister. She looked so tired, dirty and defeated. "Let her go. She's telling you the truth."

"Shut up."

Jacie's anger simmered along with her frustration. If only she could get loose.

Then what? The man had the advantage. He was stronger and probably had weapons at his disposal. Jacie might get free, but she wouldn't leave without her sister.

The man waved a finger toward the shadows. "Bring him in."

Jacie's breath lodged in her throat and she braced herself. Who was the masked man referring to? Had they captured Zach? Was he still alive?

Two hulking Hispanics with dragon tattoos on their arms dragged a man into the light.

He slumped between the two men, moaning, his dark hair hanging over his forehead, the shadows cast by the overhead light blocking his features.

Then the henchmen let go.

Their captive slumped to the floor and rolled onto his back. Both eyes were swollen and a large bruise had formed on his jaw. His clothes were torn as if he'd been whipped.

Tracie's eyes widened. "Bruce?"

The figure on the floor moaned, "Tracie."

"Your boyfriend was more forthcoming. It seems he's been busy cutting deals with both the Los Lobos and La Familia." The masked man waved a hand at the men standing nearby. "This makes *mi familia* angry."

The man closest to Bruce kicked him in the side.

Bruce groaned and tried to crawl away from him.

"What are you going to do with us?" Jacie asked, dreading the answer.

"La Familia suffers no traitors." The man stood and walked toward the door. "They're yours. Dispose of them."

IT TOOK THEM longer to get to the abandoned house than they'd anticipated because of the ominous overcast sky stealing the light of the stars and moon. Riding through the night without light proved to be more difficult than originally expected. Thunder rumbled, teasing them with the possibility of a raging storm at any moment. But the rain didn't come, which let them progress through the darkness.

They would have missed the perimeter guard altogether had Zach not slipped on the night-vision goggles when he did. Thankfully the wind had picked up. That and the thunder covered the sound of their horses and the creaking of saddle leather as they dismounted.

"You two stay here until I take care of the outlying guards."

"We can help." Richard pulled a knife from his belt. "I was in the infantry back in the day."

"I appreciate that, but I'm the only one with night-vision goggles and we can't afford to alert the rest of the camp. Once I take this man out, Richard, you move forward to where he was. I'll be circling to the right. Give me five minutes and then Humberto can take up a position a hundred yards to Richard's right. Make sure you have clearance to fire into the compound."

"But we can't see anything," Humberto pointed out.

"Once I have the guards taken care of, I'll start the fireworks. You'll be able to see into the compound and they won't be able to see out. Only fire if you're certain of what you're shooting at. My first order of business is to find the women. When I do, I'm going to create a diversion. Be ready." Zack filled a clip with rounds.

"What kind of diversion?" Richard asked.

"Something with a lot of fire and noise." Zach pressed a hand to the incendiary grenade.

When he found the women, he'd have to distract the guards long enough to free Tracie and Jacie and hopefully get them out.

"Hank's sending out his men and will be notifying the FBI and DEA about now. If they send out their helicopter, we'll have additional firepower should we run into trouble. The main thing is to get the women to safety first."

Richard nodded. "We'll cover you."

Humberto's head hung low. "I'm sorry I got Jacie involved in this."

Zach held up his hand. "Now's not the time for regrets. It's time for action."

"Sí." Humberto squared his shoulders, his lips firming into a straight line. "We're behind you."

Zach checked his web belt one last time, memorizing the location of each item of equipment. With his rifle in hand, he slipped into the night, his night-vision goggles in place.

He made straight for the man on the northern edge of the compound perimeter. As he grew close, he slipped the goggles up on his head and circled around behind the man, dispatching him with a swift, clean stroke with his knife.

One down, still more to go before he could enter the grounds and check for the women.

Zach circled the compound, moving as quickly as he could without making noise. At the western edge of the perimeter, he found one of the compound's sentries fast asleep. The man never knew what happened. He died where he lay.

Another man on the south side was easily taken care of. At least one other remained on the eastern perimeter. The green glow of his body heat registered in Zach's night-vision goggles.

As he eased toward the man, his gaze fixed on his target, Zach didn't see the rock until he kicked it with his toe.

The sound of the stone skittering across the dry soil might as well have been the blaring of a horn.

"Que hay de nuevo?" The man lifted his weapon, aiming toward Zach.

"Es mi," Zach replied with his best Spanish accent; then he slipped around to the side of the man holding the weapon aimed at the spot where Zach had kicked the rock.

"El que?" The man's voice rose.

When Zach was behind the man, he rushed forward and grabbed him from behind.

The guard struggled, his hands still on his rifle. A shot rang out.

Damn. The entire camp would be on alert now.

Zach used his knife to dispatch the man and ran back to the south side of the compound, away from where he'd dropped the last guard and where the others would be headed to discover the source and reason for the gunfire.

With the first shot having been fired, Zach's plan would have to move a little quicker than anticipated.

With only three buildings on the old ranch, Zach snuck up to the back of an old, dilapidated barn that leaned precariously, slats missing from the walls. No light streamed from inside, and a quick scan with the night-vision goggles concluded it was empty. He pushed the goggles up on his forehead. This was the spot, and it was now or never.

Footsteps pounded against the dirt, and a shout rose, followed by more and the clinking of metal against metal as men grabbed weapons and headed toward the perimeter to investigate the shots fired.

Zach pulled the incendiary grenade from the loop holding it on his web harness and yanked the pin. Then he tossed it into the old barn and slipped away in the shadows toward the next building. He threw himself to the ground, covering his ears.

Let's get this party started.

THE GOONS LEFT to "dispose" of Bruce, Tracie and Jacie chuckled as they hiked their rifles up and prepared to follow orders. They spoke to each other in Spanish, pointing first at Tracie, then Jacie and finally Bruce.

Jacie held her breath. With her hands duct-taped behind her, she was helpless to stop what was about to happen. She twisted her wrists, hoping to stretch the tape and allow enough room to pull her hands free. But they'd bound her so tightly, her hands had gone numb. She stared across the room at her sister, praying for a miracle.

The La Familia gang members raised their rifles, aimed and—

Jacie braced herself for the carnage, her gaze inexplicably drawn to one man's trigger finger as his finger tightened.

An explosion ripped through the air, shaking the ground beneath Jacie's feet.

The gunman jerked as he pulled the trigger, hitting the other gang member in the knee. The wounded man dropped to the floor, clutching his knee and screaming Spanish obscenities.

The man who'd shot him bent to him, speaking fast, then he ran to the front door and flung it open.

With her back to the door, Jacie craned her neck to see what was happening. A glow filled the night sky, reflected off the low-slung clouds.

The man on the floor struggled to his feet, using his rifle as a makeshift crutch. He hobbled to the door and out onto the porch with the other man.

"Jacie," Tracie called out. "Can you make your way over here?"

"I don't know." Jacie gathered her strength and performed a kind of sitting hop, moving herself a mere inch toward her sister.

"Again." Tracie did the same. With their legs bound to the chair legs, they couldn't get much traction, but with both of them moving forward, the distance shortened.

Her heart pounding in her ears, Jacie hurried until they were almost knee-to-knee. "Pass me on your right."

Tracie hopped past Jacie.

Once behind her, Jacie scooted her chair to the side. "Can you move your fingers at all? They used duct tape on me."

"You might have a better shot at untying me than I would at tearing the tape."

Jacie strained to reach her sister's bindings, leaning forward to tip her chair backward enough to raise her hands.

The men left to kill them were shouting at people running by.

"Wh-what's happening?" Bruce lifted his head and peered through swollen eyes at the room around him.

"We don't know, but help us," Jacie whispered, loud enough for Bruce to hear.

Bruce pushed up to his hands and knees, then collapsed again, facedown on the floor.

The men in the doorway stopped yelling and turned back to the house, guns raised.

"Jacie." Tracie spoke quietly. "We've got trouble."

THE EXPLOSION ROCKED the ground beneath Zach.

Shots rang out in the distance.

Zach prayed the guards hadn't found Richard and Humberto. For a moment, he second-guessed his decision to bring them along. They weren't trained in these kinds of operations.

Pushing aside his concern for the two men, Zach inched around the side of the small building. He stayed in the deep shadows cast by the fire growing in the barn. The grenade did its job and set the building ablaze. It wouldn't take long to burn to the ground. The ancient timbers would be easily consumed.

A man raced by, sporting an M110 similar to the one Zach carried. Where had the man gotten the American weapon?

As soon as he passed, Zach ran to the next building.

A motorcycle revved and took off out of the melee, a man wearing a black bandana and a black mask heading north, lights extinguished.

Above, thunder boomed in the night and the first drops of moisture splattered the earth.

More shots were muffled by the descending clouds.

Behind Zach, the fire grew, undaunted by a few drops of rain and building in heat and intensity. Chaos reigned.

Banking on the confusion, Zach pushed through the door of the small outbuilding. Light shone through the windows from the barn's fire. The building contained boxes and burlap sacks, but no people. With only the ranch house remaining, Zach steeled himself. He quit the smaller outbuilding and raced across the grounds.

As he neared the house, a man leaned out over the deck, his weapon pointed toward Zach. *"Que hay de nuevo?"*

Zach didn't bother answering; he shot the man and dove for the shadows, rolled to his feet and rounded the corner to the back entrance.

Another guard leaped off the back porch, heading straight for Zach.

Zach didn't give him the opportunity to ask who was there. A single bullet pierced the man's chest, downing him where he stood, leaving the back door unprotected. Zach sucked in a deep breath and nudged the door open with the nose of his rifle.

As soon as he pushed through, he dodged to the

left, out of the backlight from the burning barn. He'd entered through the kitchen. If they had the women in this house, they'd be in the living room or locked in one of the bedrooms.

Zach moved from room to room. Above the shouts and rumbling of thunder, Zach heard low thumps and scraping sounds. He headed toward the sound, stopping at a corner. There it was again. The bumping, scraping sound.

Crouching low and staying as much in the shadows as he could, Zach peeked around the wall.

Bound to chairs, Tracie and Jacie sat back to back. He recognized Jacie by the clothes she'd been wearing earlier. She faced him. A man lay sprawled across the floor. He looked vaguely like Bruce, only banged up. Standing in the front door was a large Hispanic man, wielding a semiautomatic rifle aimed at Tracie's chest. If he pulled the trigger at this close range, the bullet would cut right through Tracie and lodge in Jacie, killing both women.

His heart skipped several beats and the world whirled around him. Images of a similar style of torture flashed through him. Toni being beaten by the men of Los Lobos while he remained tied to a beam, powerless to help her.

His breathing grew shallow, his hands clammy. The hopeless feeling washing over him made his hands shake, crippling him.

"Let her live," Jacie begged. "Kill me if you must, but let my sister live."

Jacie's words rang out, cutting through the fog of Zach's memories. She wasn't Toni. Zach wasn't helpless this time. His heartbeat settled into a smooth, deadly rhythm, his hands growing steady.

Zach refused to let Jacie die. He wanted more time with the woman who'd brought him back to life—the woman who marched bravely into battle and who wouldn't give up on her sister or on him.

He tipped the nose of his rifle around the corner and lined up the sights.

Jacie's eyes rounded when she spotted him.

Zach pulled the trigger.

Chapter Sixteen

Another shot rang out.

Bruce jerked on the floor beside Jacie and moaned. Blood pooled on the floor beside him.

A loud thump was followed by a shout from the doorway.

Jacie scooted her chair halfway around so that she could see what was happening.

Zach leaped past her to the front door.

The cartel man with the wounded leg had thrown himself off the front porch into the dirt, yelling at the top of his voice.

More La Familia gang members came running toward the house.

Zach stepped back and closed the door. He yanked a blood-encrusted knife from a scabbard on his thigh.

"Look out, Jacie!" Tracie cried. "He's got a knife."

"It's okay. He's a good guy," Jacie reassured her.

Zach sliced through Jacie's bindings and then

Tracie's. "We have to get out of here before they surround us."

Jacie leaped from her chair and steadied herself on Zach's arm.

Tracie was not so fast, having been starved for the days she'd spent in captivity and beaten on multiple occasions. She stumbled to her feet and pitched forward.

Jacie and Zach grabbed for her before she fell to the floor.

Zach looped Tracie's arm over his shoulder, then tossed his pistol to Jacie.

She caught it and aimed it at the front door as Zach half dragged, half led her sister to the rear of the house.

"What about Bruce?" Tracie asked.

"Leave him. He'll slow us down," Zach said.

Jacie hated Bruce for what he'd gotten her sister into, but she knew what his fate would be if they left him with La Familia. "They'll kill him if we leave him."

Jacie followed Zach, inching backward, her gaze trained on the front of the house, torn between helping the man and getting out alive.

At any moment, La Familia Diablos could storm the house to find the people responsible for their buddy's commotion. They'd find Bruce, blame him and finish him off.

"I can't leave him. He's still alive." Jacie stopped backing up.

"He's not worth it," Zach insisted. "He's a traitor to his country."

"Yeah, but let the courts sentence him. Not La Familia." Jacie took a step back the way she'd come.

"No, Jacie! Zach's right. Saving Bruce isn't worth your getting shot." Tracie dug in her heels and stopped herself and Zach.

"Don't, Jacie. If anyone should go back, it should be me." Zach reached out and grabbed her arm. "He'll be heavy. You can't lift him on your own. Get your sister out of here."

Jacie chewed her lip. "No, I can't let you go in there."

"We don't have time to argue about it. Take my gun and get Tracie out." He looped Tracie's arm over Jacie's shoulder, pressed a kiss to Jacie's lips. "I want a real date when we get back to sanity."

Jacie's heart turned a somersault and she grinned. "You got it. Don't stand me up." Her chest squeezed hard as Zach ducked past her and back into the front room.

Jacie forced herself not to think about what he might be facing. With Tracie leaning heavily on her, she hurried through the house to the back door.

"Wait." Tracie laid her hand on the door, refusing to let Jacie go through. "There could be men outside the door. Check through the windows first."

Jacie propped Tracie against the wall and crossed to the bare window, careful not to stand behind its glass. Although it was dark in the kitchen, she couldn't take the chance of someone seeing her.

She eased her head around the window frame and peered out.

Men gathered in the yard between the barn and the house. Some faced the barn. They were talking and waving their hands at the flames leaping toward the sky, stirred by a strong crosswind.

One man faced the house. He spoke to another and pointed toward Jacie. She ducked back away from the glass, her pulse hammering. Had he seen her? Did it matter? With that many men standing out in the barnyard, they didn't have a chance of sneaking out the back door.

"We have to find another way out." Jacie helped Tracie into one of the bedrooms, eyeing the window on the far wall. It was on one of the house's sides, out of view of the barnyard and the front yard. She checked out the window for movement. That side of the house was shrouded in shadows. She watched for a full thirty seconds. Nothing moved. "Think you can make it out this window?"

"It's either that or die trying." Tracie's chin lifted. "I might need a boost from you."

"You got it." Jacie pushed and shoved the window, the old paint having congealed, sealing it shut. "I can't get it open."

Tracie slipped out of her shirt and handed it to Jacie. Her body was covered in deep purple bruises. "Wrap your arm with my shirt and break the glass."

Jacie swallowed her anger at what the cartel had done to Tracie and did as her sister directed. She kicked the glass away, praying La Familia couldn't hear the noise over the roar of the fire and the thunder of the approaching storm.

Using the shirt, Jacie cleared the glass from the windowsill. When it was safe enough, she shook out Tracie's shirt.

Her sister put it on, wincing as she raised her arms over her head. "Let's get out of here."

"Not without Zach." Jacie ran to the bedroom door, her gaze panning the empty hallway.

What was taking Zach so long? He should have Bruce and be back by now. So far no more shots had been fired close to the ranch house. Still, Jacie was worried.

Given the short amount of time she'd known Zach, she wasn't sure why she was so concerned. Other than that he made her heart beat faster and his kisses curled her toes.

She waited another minute. When he didn't appear in the doorway, Jacie returned to where her sister leaned against the wall. "We're getting you out of here." Jacie stooped to give her a boost.

"That'll be a challenge." Tracie raised her foot and stepped into Jacie's cupped hands.

Jacie sagged under her sister's weight, then pushed up with her knees and shoved Tracie through the opening. Her sister lodged halfway through, moaning as her ribs hit the windowsill.

"Hang on, I'm going to shove you out." Jacie planted one of Tracie's feet against her own shoulder and leaned into her, pushing her over the edge.

Tracie half slid, half rolled out, dropping to the ground onto the broken glass.

Jacie leaned out the window and whispered loud enough that Tracie could hear but the cartel couldn't, "Okay out there?"

"Will be," Tracie grunted, and righted herself, "as soon as you're out here too."

She hated leaving Tracie all alone. Not when her sister was so weak and barely able to hold herself up. "Lie low for a minute. I'll be right back. I'm going to see what's keeping Zach. Stay in the shadows."

"No, Jacie!" she called out.

Jacie ran for the living room. Zach had lifted Bruce off the floor, and struggled to throw him over his shoulder in a fireman's carry.

"What are you doing in here?" Zach staggered under the other man's weight and glared at Jacie. "I told you to get your sister out."

"I did, but I thought you might need help."

"Do you ever do what you're told?"

"Quit arguing, mister. There's a man headed this way." She held her gun steady. "I've got you covered, first door on the left."

"Yes, ma'am." Zach sagged under Bruce's dead-weight. The man had been beaten to within an inch of his life and had suffered a gunshot wound to his abdomen, but he still had a pulse. Much as he wanted to, Zach couldn't leave him to die at La Familia's hands.

He entered the bedroom.

Jacie entered behind him, closing the door.

Zach peered over the edge of the windowsill. "Tracie, move out of the way." With no time to spare or take it easy on the injured man, Zach shoved Bruce through the window.

Tracie did her best to cushion his fall, ending up knocked to the ground for her efforts.

Then Zach nodded to Jacie. "You next." He scooped her up and stuck her legs through the window. Jacie dropped to the ground as raindrops splattered across her cheeks.

"I think he's dead," Tracie mumbled.

Bruce lay at an awkward angle, his head cradled in her lap.

Jacie crouched beside the man and touched her fingers to his neck, searching for a pulse.

It took a moment before she felt it. But it was there and very weak.

Zach hauled himself through the window and dropped to the ground. He ran to the back corner of the house and then to the front, returning with a sigh. "We're not out of the woods yet."

"Which way?" Jacie asked.

A voice shouted from inside the house, and footsteps pounded across the wooden floors.

"Follow me and you'd better move fast." Zach grabbed Bruce's arms and yanked him up and over his shoulder. Then he ran due east, away from the house.

Jacie wrapped an arm around her sister's waist and followed Zach into the shadows. The farther they moved away from the flames of the burning barn, the less likely anyone would see them.

Unfortunately they didn't move fast enough to avoid detection.

A man called out behind them.

Zach dropped Bruce to the ground and shouted, "Get down!"

Bullets winged past them, kicking up plumes of dry Texas dust.

Jacie fell to a prone position at once, dragging Tracie down with her.

"What do we do now?" she cried. If they got

up to run, whoever was shooting at them would have an easy target. But they couldn't stay glued to the ground forever. Soon others of La Familia would join the shooter. It wouldn't be long before Zach, Jacie, Tracie and Bruce were full of lead.

"Now would be a good time for the backups to show," Zach muttered.

"We have backup?" Tracie asked.

"In a perfectly timed world, we would, but given the weather, I'm not sure the FBI and DEA can get the helicopter off the ground."

As if to emphasize Zach's point, the wind whipped across Jacie's face, twisting her hair.

Bruce lay beside Jacie, his eyes blinking open. "Tracie?"

"No, I'm Jacie," Jacie corrected.

"I'm here." Tracie took his hand and held it, tears shimmering in her eyes as she stared into Bruce's face.

"I'm sorry." Bruce coughed, spitting out blood. "Please forgive me."

"For almost getting me and my sister killed?" She shook her head. "I can't."

"I never meant to hurt you."

"Yeah, well, you did." The tears were flowing in earnest by now from swollen, bruised eyes. "I trusted you and you lied to me."

"I wanted out," he whispered. "But I knew too much. You have to believe me."

"You had two DEA agents killed." Tracie's hand smoothed over Bruce's face. "Where was the mercy? I don't even know you anymore."

"I'm still the same person," he insisted.

"You're not the same man I fell in love with."

"I didn't…" Bruce's voice gurgled, as if his lungs were taking on liquid. "I didn't order those two men killed."

"Then who did?" Tracie demanded, leaning up.

The man in the house fired on them, the bullet hitting the dirt in front of Jacie's face, kicking it up into her eyes. She blinked and rubbed the sand out.

Bruce's eyes closed, his breathing growing shallower.

"Don't you die on me." Tracie shook the man, tears flowing freely down her dirt-streaked cheeks. "The least you can do is tell me who is behind all of this."

"He's powerful," Bruce whispered.

"Was he the one interrogating us?" Tracie sucked in a deep breath.

"Yes."

"What's his name?"

"Too dangerous…FBI…can make people disappear."

"What do you mean?" Zach asked.

"Hank's wife and son…" Bruce's body shuddered and he coughed up more blood, and then settled back against the earth, his face creased in a grimace of pain.

"What does he have to do with Hank's family?" Zach demanded.

Bruce inhaled, the gurgling sound more pronounced. "Still alive."

"Where?" Zach grabbed the man by the collar.

Bruce's eyes blinked open, found Tracie's and they closed. "I loved you," he said, the words released on his last breath. His body went slack.

Tracie leaned her face against his chest, her shoulders shaking with silent sobs. "Damn you, Bruce. Damn you for everything."

Jacie's heart ached at her sister's distress.

Bruce had made some big mistakes. He'd betrayed his country and betrayed Tracie, but deep down had never stopped loving her.

Though tears welled in her eyes, Jacie refused to let them fall. She couldn't dwell on Bruce's mistakes, not when they were pinned to the ground, unable to move for fear of being hit.

Shouts rose from the barnyard. Flames climbed higher into the descending clouds.

Zach glanced over his shoulder and sighed. "I believe the cavalry has arrived."

Headlights shone in the distance from half a dozen vehicles. The advancing army had the remaining La Familia members scrambling for motorcycles and jeeps.

The man who'd pinned them apparently didn't know he was being surrounded and kept shooting random shots—some bullets hitting far too close for comfort.

Zach's cavalry pulled in to the ranch compound and skidded to a stop in the gravel. Doors flung open and men wearing flak vests and carrying guns poured out. The remaining cartel thugs were quickly killed or held up their hands in surrender.

As the last man standing, their sniper suddenly stopped shooting and spun, his weapon now aiming for whoever had entered the room behind him.

Two shots were fired. The sniper slammed against the windowsill and tipped out onto the gravel below. Another face appeared in the glassless window. A man wearing a dark cowboy hat instead of the dark gear of the FBI.

"Well, I'll be damned. Hank must have sent in his guys as well as the FBI. If I'm not mistaken, that was Ben." After a moment Zach stood. "I think that was our cue. Come on, let's see if they brought a medic." He reached down to grab Jacie's arm, hauling her to her feet.

Jacie touched her sister's shoulder. "We have to go."

"Go without me," Tracie said, her voice catching on a sob.

"Can't." Jacie shook her head. "You're a part of me. You're my sister. I could never leave you behind."

Tracie slid Bruce's head from her lap and pushed to a kneeling position. "Why did he have to go and be an idiot and play both sides?"

"Who knows what motivates different people?" Jacie answered. "For what it's worth, it sounded like he loved you."

Tracie snorted. "Apparently he loved himself more." She stood, swaying slightly.

"What I want to know is who the hell was the man in the mask?" The beast of a man who'd been so harsh to her sister and herself would forever haunt Jacie.

"I'm done with the bureau." Tracie pushed her hair back from her face, revealing more bruising.

Jacie flinched at all the damage. "What do you mean?" She cast a glance toward the vehicles crowding the compound, hoping they brought medical personnel to treat her sister's wounds.

Tracie's dried, split lips pulled back in a sneer. "What good is it to be an agent when you can't tell the good guys from the bad?"

Zach grabbed her shoulders and forced her to stare into his eyes. "The important thing to remember is that *you* are a good agent and that you are vital to this nation, to our country, to keeping us safe."

She stared into his eyes. "Who are you?"

"I'm Zach Adams." His hands dropped to his sides. "I used to be a special agent like you."

"Why did *you* quit?" Tracie asked.

"I lost hope." Zach faced Jacie. "Someone helped me find it again." He held out his hand to Jacie.

She took it, butterflies storming her belly and gooseflesh rising on her arms. The man definitely turned her inside out.

Tracie turned her bruised and battered face toward Jacie. "I feel like I missed something." She gave the hint of a smile. "Do you two know each other?"

"We didn't. Now we do." Jacie gave a shy smile.

"We can talk later." Zach slipped Tracie's arm over his shoulder. "Right now we need to have you seen by a doctor."

Jacie looped Tracie's other arm over her shoulders and together, they closed the distance between them and the vehicles parked near the burning barn and outbuilding. Floating embers landed on the house, lighting it like a tinderbox.

As the house burned, Jacie couldn't feel regret for the old structure, not when it held memories of terror and torture. She hoped never to feel that trapped and hopeless again.

ZACH'S PULSE HAD finally returned to normal. After finding Jacie and Tracie tied up and on the verge of being executed, he thought life had come to a standstill. Thank God, he'd arrived just in time. Bringing them out of that house alive had lifted a weight heavier than the current situation from his shoulders.

It was as if now he finally knew the meaning of his life. When he'd been a captive of Los Lobos and they'd tortured Toni to death, he'd asked God why he'd spared him and took her. Seeing Jacie and her sister about to be killed had brought his life back in focus. God had a purpose for him. He'd led him to Hank and this amazing woman. Zach was meant to fight for truth and justice, the fight he thought he'd joined the FBI to accomplish.

As the three staggered into the open, Hank Derringer broke away from a group of agents and cowboys.

"Zach, Jacie!" He took over for Jacie and, with Zach's help, led Tracie to the back of a Hummer. The hatch was open and a man was applying a bandage to Richard Giddings's forehead.

Zach held out a hand. "Thanks for covering me." He glanced around. "Where's Humberto?"

"Already on his way back to the Big Elk."

"Any injuries?" Zach asked.

"Humberto got off without a scratch. I would

have too, if I hadn't tripped over my two left feet and landed a face-plant in the gravel." Richard grinned at Jacie. "You don't know how happy I am to see my best field guide on her feet and alive."

"Thanks, Richard." Jacie gave the man a hug, moisture glistening in her eyes.

After a quick once-over, the medic cleaned one of Tracie's facial wounds. "Won't know what else is damaged until we get her back to the county hospital in Wild Oak Canyon and get some X-rays. Might even take her into El Paso for CAT scans."

"The county hospital," Tracie insisted. "And a hot shower, please. Then I think I could sleep for a hundred years."

Hank bundled her into another Hummer. Jacie and Zach climbed in on each side of her. As they pulled away from the ranch compound, Zach's gut clenched as the enormity of the situation hit. He'd almost lost Jacie.

The few raindrops the clouds had released did nothing to extinguish the fire that had completely consumed the house by now. Hank called ahead on his satellite phone and had the local doctor meet them at the county hospital, machines warmed and waiting.

After what seemed an interminable amount of time and X-rays, Tracie was shown to a room where she'd spend the night monitored by a competent staff. Zach insisted that the doctor look over Jacie, as well. Though she protested that she was fine and didn't need a doctor, she went with him.

Throughout Jacie's examination, Zach paced in the waiting room, clenching his fists, frustrated and angry at what Jacie and Tracie had gone through.

When she finally emerged, she smiled. "Told you I was fine. Other than an ugly bruise on my cheekbone and a split lip, I'll survive." The doctor found no signs of concussion or brain trauma from the multiple hits she'd taken at the hands of the mystery interrogator.

"I'm glad you're okay." Zach gathered her in his arms and pressed a gentle kiss to her forehead. "And for the record, you look great."

"Liar." She leaned into him, her arms circling his waist, her forehead pressed to his chest. "I'm glad it's over."

"Me too." He smoothed her hair from her forehead and tucked it behind her ear.

Jacie tipped her cheek into his open palm and pressed a kiss there. "Thank you for coming for us."

Zach's chest tightened as he stared down into her gray-blue eyes. "Wild horses couldn't keep me away."

Her gaze broke from his, her eyelids drifting

downward, hiding her emotions. "I want to see my sister."

Zach wanted to take Jacie somewhere they could be alone and hold her until his arms ached and the desperation of the past twenty-four hours abated. Instead he led her to her sister's room.

Tracie lay with her damp hair spread across her pillow, her damaged cheeks wiped clean of dirt and grime. Her eyes were closed, her face relaxed.

Jacie paused with Zach in the doorway. "I'm staying with her tonight," she whispered.

"No, you're not." Tracie's eyes blinked open.

Zach's fists clenched at all the swelling and the purple bruises.

Jacie stepped forward. "I'm not letting you out of my sight for a while."

"Yes, you are." Tracie's lips quirked upward slightly. "I know you want to help, but Hank assured me he'd have someone stand guard throughout the night. And I should be okay to leave the hospital tomorrow. You've done enough and need rest as much as I do."

"Still," Jacie sighed, "I'd feel better knowing you're okay."

"And I won't get any sleep with you hovering over me." Tracie closed her eyes. "Please, I just want to sleep."

Jacie closed the distance between them and gathered her sister's hand in hers. "Are you sure?"

Tracie sighed. "Yes, I'm sure." Her eyes edged open again. "Zach?"

Zach joined Jacie beside the hospital bed, the scents of alcohol and disinfectants making him itch to leave. "Yes."

Tracie disengaged her hand from Jacie's and held it out to Zach. "Thank you for coming to our rescue. I don't want to think about how this day could have ended." She laid his hand over Jacie's. "Now get her out of here. And you'd better be good to her, or you'll have me to contend with."

Zach laughed. "If you're anywhere near as tough as Jacie, I'll be shaking in my boots."

"Got that right." Tracie's eyelids drifted closed as though they weighed a ton. "I'll see you two in the morning."

Zach led Jacie out of the room.

Jacie cast one last glance over her shoulder. "I don't like leaving her."

"You heard her. She wants to sleep." Zach hugged her middle. "Hank assured me that Ben Harding is one of the best ex-cops you'll find. He'll make sure Tracie is safe."

Jacie leaned into Zach. "It's been a helluva day, hasn't it?"

"You were so brave."

"And stupid. If I'd stayed put when you told me to, I wouldn't have been caught."

"And I'd be dead. You saved me." In more ways

than one, and he'd spend a lifetime thanking her. "And that tracking device you had in your shoe led us to you and your sister. I'd say it worked out okay." Zach paused for a moment in the hallway of the hospital and touched a thumb to the bruising on her cheek. "I have to admit, though, it was a little too close for comfort." He kissed her cheek, careful not to apply too much pressure. His mouth moved to her lips.

"Ouch." Jacie backed away.

"Sorry." Zach straightened. "Did I tell you I'm really glad you're okay?"

"Yes, you did." She laughed up at him. "Do we have rides back to the Big Elk?"

"Hank let us have use of the Hummer. He'd like to see us tomorrow if you're up to it."

"Ask me tomorrow. Right now I just want to go home to bed." Her hand slipped into his and they walked out of the hospital.

The drive back to the Big Elk Ranch was accomplished in silence.

At first Zach thought Jacie had fallen asleep, she was so quiet. But a glance at her face proved him wrong. Jacie stared straight ahead, her eyes open, her bottom lip captured between her teeth.

When they pulled up in front of her little cottage, Zach leaped down and rounded to the passenger side of the vehicle to help her down. He walked her to her door. "You know, we never did have a chance to put your cabin back together."

Jacie's shoulders sagged. "I'll manage."

"You could stay in mine," he offered, turning her to face him.

Jacie's gaze rose to meet his. "I don't know if I can keep my distance."

"I'm counting on that."

"I don't know if I want to get any closer to you. Now that it's all over, I'm afraid you'll be gone tomorrow." Her eyes filled with moisture, the blue-gray of her irises swimming. "I almost lost you today to a bullet. I'm not strong enough to lose you again."

"You're not going to lose me." He slipped his hands beneath her legs and scooped her up into his arms. "I want that first real date and a lot more after that."

"Are you sure? I thought you didn't want a lasting relationship. And I won't settle for less."

"I was wrong, and for once, we're in agreement." He strode across the yard to his cabin and twisted the key in the doorknob while balancing her in his arms. "A little help here?"

"Not until you answer one question."

"Fire away."

"Do you think you could ever love me like you loved Toni?"

Zach stood still, his gaze captured by hers. Then he shook his head. "No."

Tears welled in Jacie's eyes. "Put me down. I can't do this."

He refused to let her go, his hands tightening around her. "Hear me out."

"I refuse to fall in love with someone who can't love a second time. It's hopeless."

"I don't think so." He laughed, the vibrations of his chest warming her. "I can't love you like I did Toni because you're a different person. Sure, I loved Toni. She was my partner. I'd give anything to have been able to save her life. We were a team."

"See? I can't compete with that. I'm just a trail guide."

"And a very beautiful and courageous one at that." He brushed a kiss across her undamaged cheek. "You never gave up. You taught me that anyone can make a difference, if they care enough."

"I didn't make a difference. *You* saved us." Her brow furrowed. "Put me down. I need to be alone."

He shook his head. "You made the difference, Jacie. You saved me, not only from that gunman at Enrique's place, but from myself." He held her tighter. "I could very well be falling in love with you, something I thought I could never do again."

Her eyes widened. "You're falling in love with me?" She squeaked and grasped his cheeks between her palms, her frown deepening. "But I thought you couldn't love me like you did Toni."

"I can't love you like Toni because you're Jacie. I'm falling in love with you, if you'll give me a chance."

Her eyes filled with tears, and a smile spread across her face. "So what's keeping you?"

He laughed and pushed the door open to the cabin. "I don't want to make any rash decisions when we've known each other less than a week."

"Ever heard of love at first sight?" Jacie tipped her head. "Or in our case, maybe it was second or third sight."

Zach set her on her feet and pulled her into his arms. "Whatever, I want to spend time getting to know you better."

"Now you're talking." Jacie pushed the door closed behind him, shutting the world out and them in.

Epilogue

Hank leaned against the front of his desk. "Zach, thank you for helping Jacie and Tracie out of a tight situation. I knew you were the right man for the job, and you didn't disappoint."

Zach held tight to Jacie's hand. "I'm glad I could help. Thanks for the opportunity." His gaze was on Jacie, not Hank.

"Although we didn't get the man behind it all, at least we uncovered one of the moles in the FBI."

Tracie sat in a wingback leather chair, her color returning, though her eyes seemed dull and unhappy. "I wish I'd known sooner about Bruce's activities."

"What would you have done that you didn't do once you learned of them?" Jacie asked.

Tracie stared at her hands. "I wouldn't have fallen for all his lies."

"The thing to remember is that you stayed true to your country and your duty as an FBI agent. I commend you on your spirit and desire to seek justice and truth." Hank drew in a deep breath and opened his mouth to go on. "Which brings me to—"

Zach held up his hand. "Don't you think Tracie makes a perfect FBI agent?"

Hank smiled. "I guess you know I was about to offer her a position?"

Tracie shook her head. "Although I'm disappointed that some of our agents are bad, I'm not giving up on the bureau. I still believe in it and what we can do to preserve justice in this country. Between you, Zach and Jacie, you reminded me of what an honor it is to serve."

Hank waved a hand. "If you decide to retire from the bureau, please consider my team."

Tracie smiled and nodded. "You bet I will."

Hank turned to Jacie. "What about you? You're quite a good shot, brave and a seeker of truth and justice—"

Jacie held up her hand. "Though I know I could do the danger thing in a pinch, it's not for me. I like leading hunting parties and promoting the Big Elk Ranch."

Zach squeezed her hand.

Warmth flushed her neck and cheeks at the memories of all the places those hands had been throughout the night and halfway through the morning. "Thanks, but I think I'll stay where I am."

"That leaves you, Zach. I consider the job you

did a trial on your part and mine. I'm convinced you will be a valuable asset to this organization. Care to continue?"

Zach nodded. "If Jacie has no objections, I'm in."

Jacie raised her hand. "No objections here, as long as I get to see you between jobs."

"Then that's settled. I have my contacts searching for the leader of the stateside La Familia gang that held you two ladies. Until then, stay on your toes in case he seeks retribution."

"One other thing, Hank," Zach interrupted. "Before Bruce died, he mentioned the man was powerful with connections in the FBI. Bruce said that he could make people disappear. He mentioned your family. He intimated that they may still be alive."

Hank's face blanched and he closed his eyes, dragging in a deep breath. "Any clue as to where he's keeping them?"

"Sorry, Bruce died before he could say more than that. He didn't know a location or in what condition they were."

Zach didn't want to think about what physical state Hank's wife and child would be in. Given the mystery man's propensity for pain, it couldn't be good.

His arm slipped around Jacie's shoulders. "I'll do anything in my power to help you find him and bring him down. After what he did to Jacie and Tracie, the man deserves to die."

Hank rose from his seat, crossed the room and held out his hand to Zach.

Zach stood and gripped the outstretched hand.

"Thank you, Zach," Hank said. "I'll be taking you up on that offer."

* * * * *

Don't miss Elle James's next romance,
BODYGUARD UNDER FIRE,
available September 2013 from
Harlequin Intrigue.

LARGER-PRINT BOOKS!
GET 2 FREE LARGER-PRINT NOVELS PLUS
2 FREE GIFTS!

HARLEQUIN
INTRIGUE®

BREATHTAKING ROMANTIC SUSPENSE

YES! Please send me 2 FREE LARGER-PRINT Harlequin Intrigue® novels and my 2 FREE gifts (gifts are worth about $10). After receiving them, if I don't wish to receive any more books, I can return the shipping statement marked "cancel." If I don't cancel, I will receive 6 brand-new novels every month and be billed just $5.49 per book in the U.S. or $5.99 per book in Canada. That's a saving of at least 13% off the cover price! It's quite a bargain! Shipping and handling is just 50¢ per book in the U.S. and 75¢ per book in Canada.* I understand that accepting the 2 free books and gifts places me under no obligation to buy anything. I can always return a shipment and cancel at any time. Even if I never buy another book, the two free books and gifts are mine to keep forever.

199/399 HDN F42Y

Name	(PLEASE PRINT)

Address	Apt. #

City	State/Prov.	Zip/Postal Code

Signature (if under 18, a parent or guardian must sign)

Mail to the **Harlequin®** Reader Service:
IN U.S.A.: P.O. Box 1867, Buffalo, NY 14240-1867
IN CANADA: P.O. Box 609, Fort Erie, Ontario L2A 5X3

**Are you a subscriber to Harlequin Intrigue books
and want to receive the larger-print edition?
Call 1-800-873-8635 today or visit www.ReaderService.com.**

* Terms and prices subject to change without notice. Prices do not include applicable taxes. Sales tax applicable in N.Y. Canadian residents will be charged applicable taxes. Offer not valid in Quebec. This offer is limited to one order per household. Not valid for current subscribers to Harlequin Intrigue Larger-Print books. All orders subject to credit approval. Credit or debit balances in a customer's account(s) may be offset by any other outstanding balance owed by or to the customer. Please allow 4 to 6 weeks for delivery. Offer available while quantities last.

Your Privacy—The Harlequin® Reader Service is committed to protecting your privacy. Our Privacy Policy is available online at www.ReaderService.com or upon request from the Harlequin Reader Service.

We make a portion of our mailing list available to reputable third parties that offer products we believe may interest you. If you prefer that we not exchange your name with third parties, or if you wish to clarify or modify your communication preferences, please visit us at www.ReaderService.com/consumerschoice or write to us at Harlequin Reader Service Preference Service, P.O. Box 9062, Buffalo, NY 14269. Include your complete name and address.

HILP13R

ReaderService.com

Manage your account online!

- Review your order history
- Manage your payments
- Update your address

---

*We've designed
the Harlequin® Reader Service
website just for you.*

Enjoy all the features!

- Reader excerpts from any series
- Respond to mailings and special monthly offers
- Discover new series available to you
- Browse the Bonus Bucks catalog
- Share your feedback

Visit us at:

ReaderService.com